PUS

Pe ple
Know
It's Me

'The inimitable soul of Naples is at the very heart of this astonishing book. One of the strongest of the season'

CORSE MATIN

'Benvenuto crafts her writing, chiselling page after page with an unusual narrative voice, rich ideas and surprising turns . . . illuminates and unfolds new spaces for an existence too often ignored'

IL MANIFESTO

'A flowing novel that can be read in one breath . . . immerses the reader in the life and thoughts of someone who was forced to grow up too quickly'

IL GIORNALE LOCALE

'Highly original and surprising'

LA GAZZETTA DI SAN SEVERO

'A dark tale set in the juvenile prison of Nisida . . . where readers will not only find horror but also – paradoxically – dignity and pride'

IL NAPOLISTA

Author photo
© Sugirthan Baskaran

FRANCESCA MARIA BENVENUTO was born in Naples. She graduated with a Law degree and completed a PhD in International Criminal Law. In 2012, she moved to Paris to study for a Master's Degree in Criminal Law at the Sorbonne. She then started her own law firm in Paris, where she currently works as a criminal lawyer. Her debut novel, *So People Know It's Me*, was published in Italy by Mondadori.

ELIZABETH HARRIS is a translator of literary Italian fiction based in Minneapolis. She has been awarded an NEA Translation Fellowship, the Italian Prose in Translation Award, and the National Translation Award.

So People Know It's Me

Francesca Maria Benvenuto

TRANSLATED FROM THE ITALIAN
BY ELIZABETH HARRIS

PUSHKIN PRESS

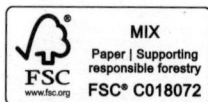

Pushkin Press
Somerset House, Strand
London WC2R 1LA

So People Know It's Me was first published as
L'amore assaje by Mondadori in Milan, 2024

First published by Pushkin Press in 2025

ISBN 13: 978-1-80533-174-2

A CIP catalogue record for this title is available from the British Library

The authorised representative in the EEA is
eucomply OÜ, Pärnu mnt. 139b-14, 11317, Tallinn, Estonia,
hello@eucompliancepartner.com, +33757690241

Designed and typeset by Tetragon, London
Printed and bound in the United Kingdom by Clays Ltd, Elcograf S.p.A.

Pushkin Press is committed to a sustainable future for our
business, our readers and our planet. This book is made from
paper from forests that support responsible forestry.

MIX
Paper | Supporting
responsible forestry
FSC® C018072
www.fsc.org

www.pushkinpress.com

1 3 5 7 9 8 6 4 2

For my mom and dad

"People place more value on life than anything else—funny, when you consider all the good things there are in this world."

ROMAIN GARY,
The Life Before Us

There's a *survegliante* on my wing who's a real zero, and that's the truth.

His name's Costantino and he's barely got any teeth. Just two in his whole head.

He's butt ugly.

A *survegliante*'s what you on the outside would call a guard, but to me he's a *survegliante*.

You see what I'm saying?

So I made this promise to Mrs Martina, our teacher here in Nisida. Our Italian teacher.

I promised to write down what I'm thinking, get it on paper.

She says if I do, she'll say nice stuff about me to the Warden so I'll get a furlough at Christmas. Two days, almost two whole days: evening on the 24th, and then the 25th.

But then she reads it for me, to make sure it's clear.

So I'm telling you right now, someone's correcting me after. Cause I'm no cheater.

In my life, I've stole, dealt, even killed somebody, but I never cheated nobody, cause I got my pride and most of all my honor.

And this is the only way I know how to talk.

So, Teach, let's get things straight.

I'll write everything you want me to. Then you have who you want read it.

But leave in a couple mistakes, so people know it's me.

It's important it's me.

If not, I won't know myself when I look in the mirror.

You do the commas, though.

I don't know how to do the commas, you know I don't like them.

Periods got more pride.

So my name's Zeno. A strange name — *'nu nomm' strano*.

First cause it starts with Z that's last in the alphabet.

If it was up to me, I'd of chose something better, something scary, Rambo, maybe, something American.

Or something starting with A, cause A's always first, so that makes it best.

But then, Teach, you told me Zeno's nice. That it's out of a book, some famous character, some guy who smokes and smokes and smokes, just like me, and he never quits, though he tries like crazy.

Poor guy, he's worse off than me.

But I'm not trying to quit, cause I look good when I smoke, plus if I don't got a cigarette, I don't know what to do with my hands. Been smoking since I was eleven.

You also said I had to read the book about "Zeno who smokes," and that I need to quit smoking, cause it's bad for me.

Not now though. I don't got the time. Some other time I'll read it. Promise. Don't worry.

So I'm in here, the opposite of out there.

I'm in the Nisida Juvenile Detention Center cause I killed somebody, shot him, that is.

I mean, you don't need a gun to kill somebody, there's knives, or your bare hands, or you can wear gloves, or there's bombs, or you can kick somebody in the head. Plenty of choices to kill somebody. Not so many to die.

I fired three times, just sorta at him and he fell over, all bloody.

I was on my scooter and it was crazy hot out. I escaped into Forcella, but they caught me cause everybody saw me—it was morning.

They picked me up on Vico Carbonari. And they went and told my mom a few hours later, without me there.

I don't know the dead guy's name, maybe he had a good name, better than mine.

He wanted to shoot me and I did it first, cause I know how to use a piece, but I can't tell you who taught me.

When I got here, the prison penguin, the nun, she told me it was pointless to kill him cause now he was free and I was in jail.

But you tell me: who should die first, me or him?

So I told this penguin: "You don't know he's free! Maybe there's prisons after, what do you know, Nun, you're not dead. You're still alive, unfortunately. So go screw yourself."

That upset the penguin pretty good and she said to find out about "after," I had to talk with Don Vicienzo, the prison priest. But he's a liar, that guy, he's always talking crap.

12

"After," to me, is what there is when you die.

And no one knows, not even priests. No one's ever been, but people just make up a bunch of stupid shit anyway.

So I really don't give a shit about after, Teach.

Just think about now. That's good enough for me.

They put me in Nisida, and I really don't like it, cause it's an island. Like Sicily, only littler and no cities.

I wanted to be in Santa Maria Capua Vetere. It's on a road, not the water.

In Santa Maria Capua Vetere I could get out all the notes I want, throw them out the window, and someone could toss answers back at me from the sidewalk.

I could even keep up my business—but I ain't writing about that.

I could send kisses to my Natalina, my girlfriend—I'll tell you more about her later!

But they put me in here, on this isolated island.

I told the Warden if a place opens up in Santa Maria Capua Vetere they should transfer me, not Totore, cause he's a bastard and don't deserve it.

Plus, Totore goes home next year.

Me, I got a good two and a half years left in here, by the sea, with all the other juvies, cause I'm fifteen.

After that, you'll send me to Poggioreale Prison—August 3, 1994, to be exact—and you know it too, Boss. Cause that's what's written down, and things written down are a real bitch. Nice gift they'll get me for my birthday, huh? When I'm legal.

The sea's useless here at Nisida.

What's useful for us is what we can really use, otherwise we might as well just go and kill ourselves, and that ain't fair.

And you won't even let us swim in the sea, cause you think we'll try and escape!

So we only get to look at it.

Me, I don't know how to swim, I swear. I don't want to escape. Just get wet, is all. Use a raft, those floaty things.

Boss, if you read this, and a place opens up at Santa Maria Capua Vetere, keep me in mind, I'm always available.

Mom was a whore.

Sorry, everybody. But Teach, you know it's the truth and I have to say it plain, cause that was her job and I don't know how else to put it.

Maybe these things'll upset somebody, I don't know.

If I got to tell it all, though, I can't hide Mom was a whore, cause it's important.

And in the end, it's a job, and my mom's always kept her pride.

I don't know if she's still one, or else maybe she quit. She's getting old, and men don't look at her dirty now, they look at her sad.

My mom didn't want to be a whore, I mean, cause there are girls who always wanted to, but I don't judge nobody — just do your thing.

My mom, though, let's be straight, she had to become one when my dad went to jail. Had to, for us, her kids, I mean.

And it's not just her out there in the *vicoli*.

In Forcella, where we live, there's a lot of whores and it's not like you can hide it.

You see a whole bunch of them out there.

They're standing around, each by their building, at their regular time. Everybody knows them, even little kids. But the ones who know them best live in the rich neighborhoods. These guys pretend like they don't know whores exist. They tell everybody all that exists is mom-women and wife-women.

But that ain't true.

Everybody knows there's something else besides.

And I'm fine with my mom being something else besides and that she does all three together.

She hasn't sent me word since I been in here, over a year now.

But Teach, you told me I can go home two days at Christmas, the evening of the 24th and the 25th, and that's so great, cause it means she didn't forget me.

You're always saying nobody ever forgets their kids.

But that ain't true, cause time passes even for moms and everybody's got their own life and their own problems. You always got your daughter right there keeping an eye on her, so you can't forget her.

But not my mom.

Maybe first she forgets one of my eyes, then the other, then my nose, legs, arms, till she has to put me back together again inside her head. I hope she looks at my photo sometimes so she can remember me.

But my father, I really don't give a fuck if he remembers me.

I don't know where he is now.

No, the truth is I do know, and so do you.

Everybody knows.

The social worker in here—she's stupid—she's always saying I should write my dad.

A letter.

So I pretend I don't know how to write. And please don't say no different. Teach, you said the social worker's stupid too, but this time she's also right. So I promised I'd write him a letter.

But not now.

Before he was in Poggioreale, then they put him in Bergamo, still in jail, never out.

I never heard of Bergamo.

But it's up there, in Northern Italy, you told me, and it's windy and foggy and cold.

You said it's awful in the North.

You think it sucks up there, huh?

I got a sister who was a whore too, for a little while, not too long, and then she just ended up a wife.

I can't tell you the guy's name she married. I could get killed if I do. Let's call him Baldy.

Him I can't stand. I didn't go to the wedding, my mom neither—we weren't invited.

Baldy told my sister—her name's Vittoria—that when I get out she's not allowed to talk to me.

But I don't give a shit, and I'm talking to her even if he says no.

Before this guy, I took care of Vittoria and Mom, with my business.

And *ringraziando 'a Maronna*, I had my spot right in the *vicoli* and I could defend my mom and sister, her name's Vittoria, I think I already said and if not, I'm saying it now.

Mom gave us kind of noble names.

But them names didn't count for nothing. Noble names don't make you noble—they don't get you no castle—for that you need money, and that we ain't got.

So there was four of us, then three, then two, and now it's just my mom.

Mom and Dad met when they were kids living outside Piscinola, in the country. They were dirt poor, poorer than we are now. Mom stole tangerines off the trees. And Dad stole garlic and onions. They sold them at the market. And that's where they met the first time. And fell in love.

So they start hanging out together, you know, messing around, bed stuff.

But they're too young for that and their families want to slit their throats, and I can understand why.

When Mom learned she was pregnant with Vittoria, she was super young, more of a baby than that baby in her belly.

So the two of them, they run off to Piscinola, otherwise their relatives would of killed them for sure, specially my mom. And they don't got nothing, just four thousand lire, some potatoes, and love, and love you can't eat.

They went to Forcella. They knew someone in the *vicoli* who could get Dad some work. And Dad became what he had to, no way around it.

In Forcella, we lived in a real *zuzzuso* shithole.

Can't really call it an apartment, but for those living there it was. With a door, a bed, two chairs, and a table. Not ours, cept one of the chairs. The rest is Adriano Santacroce's, he's a loan shark.

I don't really know our address.

It's on a *vicolo*, I don't know if there's numbers. Definitely no number on our place, on account of it's illegal.

So city hall thinks we don't exist, but that ain't true: we exist like all the others and then some, but the mayor don't give a shit and pretends he's blind.

Before everything changed, we slept all four of us in the same bed.

Now Vittoria sleeps with that bastard in his bed.

Dad's in Bergamo.

I'm here.

And Mom's alone, still in that shithole.

And she's getting old, I know it.

But *che ce putimm' fa'*?

Time does its own thing, it don't care if you're a decent person or not. Way I see it, though, there's no shame in getting old, happens to everybody. And my mom's a good age now, not too old, not too young.

She's a real good woman.

We always got hugs and kisses and a good whipping besides, cause she had to be a dad too, even though she's a woman.

If you talk to my mom, Teach, please tell her I still love her.

Even if we don't see each other.

And even if she is getting old.

Cause that ain't her fault.

In here, we don't got friends — it ain't allowed.

They think we'll start a revolt, that we'll all join together and pound the shit out of the guards.

We pretend to hate each other. But we got our groups.

We're good to each other, inside our groups. Outside, no.

But some of those guys I really love, like you do your regular friends.

Like Marietto, him I love, and also Corradino, the *femminiell'* — the tranny — who we all call *'o fecat'*, but that's a real filthy word you shouldn't say.

These guys I protect, they're my bunkies. No one messes with them — they do, they deal with me.

Then there's others I hate for real, and I don't have to pretend. No need.

Like Totore, who I hate, the guards hate, all the boys hate, and the teachers too.

Him, I'd spit in his face any day of the week.

You know Totore, Teach. He's got the sex disease, and that we can't accept. All of us got moms, sisters.

At least an aunt.

He's a perv, hurts girls. And he's only fifteen years old, like me!

And along with Totore, a little less than him, I can't stand the *surveglianti*.

Well, not all of them, some are actually pretty decent, for being guards.

Franco's the best of them. He's somewhere between forty and sixty.

He's real tall, mountain tall. My mom's always saying: "Being tall is almost all!" But even if Franco's tall, he's ugly as a clogged toilet.

But he's a good guy—*'nu brav' omm'*.

Franco, his dad was a criminal, but Franco decided to clean up his act. Did you know that, Teach? His father also killed a guy, maybe more than one.

Don't tell nobody. He's ashamed. Plus telling somebody's secrets would make me a real zero, and I'd never do that!

Franco likes to help out "the next guy," and in here "the next guy" is us, the prisoners.

He could of decided to help out "the next guy" in church, like the priests, but Franco don't really believe. It's all just superstition, cause you can't ever really know. But he still keeps a rosary in his pocket just in case, security against the *maluocchio*.

Franco's studied to be inside, without chains, kinda like you, Teach.

But you studied way more than him, cause you talk better and you know more. You studied a lot! Franco's got way less school. He speaks Neapolitan, just like us.

He's ashamed of his dad and his past. He won't talk about it. With me he does, though. He's always telling me how his dad was in jail, and how he died there.

He tells me a person's not obliged to commit crimes, even if your dad does. He says I can change my ways, clean up my act, and it don't even take soap.

But I told him I like my job, though no offense to his.

And that's the truth.

I don't do it cause my dad did. I chose. And I'm way better at it than him.

You don't agree, Teach. You're always telling me they "turned" me.

But that ain't true.

Nobody turned me.

I got my pride.

But other than Franco, on my cell wing there's a *survegliante* named Costantino and he's a real piece of shit, like I told you already.

He's the worst of them. Even if he croaked he'd be bad, with that black soul of his.

Costantino belongs in a horror movie.

He's got eyes like sewer drain holes.

He don't work here cause he loves anything about it, cept taking it out on us.

He swears at us, hits us, kicks the living shit out of

us. Sometimes he'll spit right in our face, it's completely gross—who does he think he is?

Teach, you're always saying we need to report what he does to the Warden, that they're still crimes, even if they're committed against us.

But what's the point, Teach?

For me, Costantino's the very worst of them, worse than all the others—cause he can't take that I killed somebody.

When he was young, his brother was killed in a knife fight near Pallonetto.

Franco told me.

Sorry, but what's that got to do with me?

Did I kill his brother?

I wasn't even born yet!

But he don't give a shit I wasn't even born yet, it's still my fault his brother died.

So Costantino, every time I walk by, he sings a song to Jesus about making me disappear:

> *Oh mio dolce Nzareno, fa' che non veda più Zeno.*
> *Oh mio dolce Gesù, fa' che Zeno non ci sia più.*

I'd like to smash his face in, this Costantino, but I can't do that—it'd just make things worse.

When he sings that song, though, I always make sure and scratch my balls.

I started stealing when I was ten.

I know this upsets you, Teach, but it's the truth.

I was good at stealing. Cars, tires, rims, radios. Never broke into houses though. Not my specialty.

Then when I got a little bigger, another thing I did was holdups.

It was Ciccio 'o Fetus' who learned me how to use a gun. He's older, lives in Forcella, but don't tell nobody.

He liked to learn the little kids cause it made him feel important. A person always feels powerful, learning others, don't you think, Teach?

You asked me a while back if it was worth it, all the crimes I done in my life.

I wasn't sure, and I didn't answer right away.

But then you told me how much you make coming here every day, teaching us and sweating blood to do it.

Peanuts!

Pathetic.

But that's not on you—you got nothing to be ashamed of! It's the ones paying you should be ashamed.

You said it was the State.

So the State should be ashamed then.

You, you work super hard and it's also your passion. But how do you feed your daughter off so little? Let me know if there's something we can do. I still got a bunch of people I know on the outside, so I can find some job for your husband, if you want.

Me, when I was on the outside, what you make in a month I lifted in two days practically. Sometimes even less.

So all told, you better believe it: them crimes was definitely worth it!

Sure they were.

Plus, I stole nice stuff.

I got a good eye.

For instance, Teach, those earrings you were wearing, maybe a year ago?

The gold ones, dangly, round, you remember?

Those were real, I know they were. Real pearls, real gold. High quality stuff.

And I asked you about them and you lied, cause we didn't know each other back then and you thought I was bad.

You said it was costume jewelry.

But that ain't true.

If we were on the outside, me and you, in Forcella, I'd of cut your ears right off your head and fuckin took em.

But not out of meanness—that was my job.

So it's just as well we met in here, Teach.

NOVEMBER 2, 1991, AND THE DEAD

Today's the dead.

I mean, it's a day made for them and the living better shut up.

I never understood why we got to celebrate the death of our dead people, yours, theirs, the whole world's, all of them together, like it's some kind of competition.

Nobody I know kicked it in November. In my family, all we got is summer dead.

But Corradino's crazy about this holiday. His mom's dead. He says this is a beautiful day to remember all the spirits, not leaving nobody out: killed people, old people, young people, little babies, women, men, trannies.

Corradino's always talking about ghosts and dead people.

In our cell, under his bed, he's got a bunch of photos of saints and Madonnas—*Maronne*—and photos of the dead, from when they were still alive. He's also got this statue of a baldy saint, and nothing personal, but him I don't like.

Corrado prays a ton, like it's some kind of sport.

And he also reads cards and palms and eyes.

And he's real good at telling you what your dream means, even if it's super strange.

He's fifteen, same as me. But Corrado's getting out soon, next February. Not me.

Corrado can't live on the girls' wing cause he's got the wrong thing between his legs.

Corrado wanted to be born a girl, but God gave him this nice package that you can't get rid of so easy.

Definitely born a guy.

When I found a good job in prison, I got a deck of Neapolitan cards.

Stole them off the guards.

And gave them to Corrado, so he could tell people's fortunes, cause that's something he likes.

But the deck was missing the ace of clubs and the five of swords. So we put in Panini *calcio* cards of Ciro Ferrara and Maradona. Corradino says they're just as good, better even than regular cards, and worth a lot more too.

Carrado's from Pompei. Not old Pompei with all the lava—new Pompei with all the *Camorristi*. And the head of the Camorra is Corradino's father.

His name's Totonno Palumbo.

And if you ain't heard of him, it means you're respectable.

Everywhere inside of Naples and out they're scared of him. He's a butcher, and he's the boss. In charge of a shitload of trafficking and fencing and other crimes. Of everybody inside, it's Corradino who's got the most dangerous and powerful blood.

Outside, he was the real deal, a big-time criminal, *l'omm gruoss*, not like me, I'm just a worker. He'd walk side by side with his father, down the streets of Pompei, and everybody when they saw them would say hello, even if they'd never been introduced.

But Corradino likes boys, same way I like girls.

And Totonno Palumbo could never accept that. He had it in for fags, Blacks too, and Chinese, and women (he messed around on his wife) and sometimes he had it in for Albanians, depending on who.

So Corradino hid it and he was so good at hiding it, he almost convinced himself he wasn't one.

But then he saw this boy selling fish in Pompei. I don't know this kid's name, Corradino says he forgot, but that can't be true—how could it?

There was no hiding it once Corradino got together with this kid. It was love that got him into trouble, love comes at you from all sides and you don't know what to do with yourself.

When Totonno Palumbo got wind of it, he wanted to gut them both. The fish boy ran away, started living on the streets in Naples, and disappeared.

But Corradino stayed put, and to keep him from getting his throat cut, his mom, Carmela, turned him in.

She went to the police and said: "My son's a piece of shit drug dealer." She's the reason her son's in jail. No one inside Nisida could touch him.

But when word got out around Pompei that she turned him in, Carmela wound up dead, shot in the face, and no one knows who did it. Well, course everybody knows.

Corrado was already on the island.

Couldn't even go to the funeral. Couldn't say goodbye. So he's got this special connection to death.

Sometimes he talks to the dead and it scares the shit out of us.

But it's not cause he's nuts, this is normal talk for him, like the dead person's one of us, or you.

He sees this dead person wandering around Nisida, going up and down the stairs. But he never says what they're like, if they're wearing something or naked, if they're a woman or a man, if their hair's long or if they're bald. He just sees them and goes: "Dead's dead and that's that."

Franco says Corradino's got special powers, and he had an aunt like that too: she could tell the future and saw ghosts.

So every week he wants Corrado to read his cards.

Cause Franco's got a whole mess of troubles.

He lists them for us every morning when he unlocks our cell. Says it makes him appreciate the little things more every day.

But I'm kind of sick of Franco's troubles.

We know them by heart now.

He's got:

cholesterol

a son, Pino, and they don't get along

a mortgage

a wife who's cheating on him.

Corradino's patient with Franco, though, cause he loves him so much. So every week he reads Franco's cards. And always gives him good news.

You ask me, he's lying just to make Franco happy.

Sometimes there's an upside-down card, and when there's one of those, it ain't supposed to bring great news. It's supposed to be twisted.

But Corrado always says no. It might be upside down, he says, but the cards are good and Franco's going to solve his problems.

Maybe not all at once.

One at a time.

He says this to keep Franco from getting scared.

Sometimes, Corrado also reads the sky, stars, planets, all that.

August 10 is supposed to be the night of shooting stars, but they don't have to, cause nobody's forcing them.

Corradino stood at our cell window to make some wishes, he's crazy into this stuff.

He kept looking and looking but the stars never fell, like they were doing it on purpose!

I went over and kept him company cause he felt so bad.

Then Marietto came over too and we watched them stars together to see if maybe one'd feel sorry for us and drop.

Nothin.

Not one stinking star kicked it.

And, Teach, even if they did fall, where'd they go anyway? Probably right into some guy's pocket who don't deserve it!

I'm young but I'm also kinda old.

Depends how you talk to me or look at me.

But a long time ago, I was *piccirillo* for real, meaning, like kids are, real kids. I don't remember back then — better that way — cause Dad used to beat me so much.

But then I got bigger and remembered everything, specially the punches.

I remember we didn't have many toys cause we didn't have any money.

All I had was a Super Santos soccer ball.

I kicked it against the wall to our place, like I was Pelé. And I'd play against two other little shits like me. We'd see who could make the most pieces fall out of the wall.

One time the cops came and told us, me and these two other kids, that we were born for prison, and in the end they were right.

So I was little for real only once, a long time ago, when I had a ball.

Then I had to grow up.

I grew up when I was ten, to be exact.

I was lucky—where I live, there's kids who grow up at five.

When Dad went to jail, first in the South and then in the North, never in the Middle, I took on my responsibilities, and I never been a kid since. And I don't play around.

I had to think about my family. I couldn't just leave Mom and my sister with no money and a bunch of troubles.

Lucky for me I found a job and Vittoria married that guy I told you about, who's bald and fat as a pig, but he does take care of her and they got a good life.

While me and Mom, our life was shit.

That guy, Vittoria's husband, he makes me and my mom sick, even if we are wretched.

That's what he called us, "wretched," like it was a word he invented just for us.

But not cause we commit crimes.

Old Baldy, he commits them too. More than us.

His are just better, is all. Rich people crimes.

So he gets by better and thinks he's worth more than us, specially me, since I snatch purses and sell drugs.

Vittoria didn't even go to my trial.

Mom asked Vittoria's husband to pay for a good lawyer for me. But he said I deserved the maximum sentence and a two-lire lawyer, and that's how it turned out.

Vittoria's already got two kids with this dirtbag.

So my mom's become a grandma, and she's still so young! Maybe younger than you, Teach, and you're still just a mom.

And I'm an uncle, but I don't count, cause I'm in here.

And I don't know if we're still sons and brothers and uncles in here, or if now we're nothing to nobody.

Mom raised me like a regular kid but maybe she shouldn't of.

Maybe she should of learned me to be crazy and stupid, cause then I wouldn't be criminally liable, the judge would say I'm unfit and put me in a mental hospital.

And then they'd let me out early and I'd be free.

For example, on our wing we got this kid Rinuccio who lost his mind a while back.

He's been in here a few months, but he's only staying a year and that's it.

Here's his problem: Rinuccio's got two heads. One's normal and the other's mental.

Next year, after he's done his time, they'll put him in some kind of psychiatric home to treat his thoughts.

Sometimes we find him walking around the wing and he's got his hand up, like he wants to say hello to somebody.

And when we go, "What's up, Rinù? Who you saying hello to?" he gives us a dirty look and says we're stupid, he ain't saying hello to nobody! He's waving the tram down, cause he needs to get to Piazza Dante.

And Rinù, he waits and waits, but that tram never ever goes by!

My trial lawyer never said I was crazy like Rinuccio.

The opposite.

That guy said I was happy, smart, "full of hope," but that ain't true, Teach.

And I don't think even he believed it, and you could tell.

Then the lawyer started going off on my family and my neighborhood.

He said it right to the judges' faces: "That Zeno Iaccarino was born and grew up in the middle of Forcella, a real shithole, where there ain't no playground or park or nothing."

And the truth is, the lawyer was right about this.

Then he said: "Poor Zeno never got no presents."

And he was right about this—also totally true.

But then he ended with something awful: "Zeno, his family didn't love him enough and so he wound up like you see him now, a criminal in jail!"

And then I wanted to spit in that lawyer's face, him and all his kind, cause my mom always made sure I never wanted for nothing, specially love!

But he didn't get it, this lawyer.

Cause he thinks love's other things.

That it's presents and tasty restaurants and gold!

That guy, he don't know love ain't rich, that love's a beggar like me.

And not like him and them judges, maybe.

And then he told everybody I wasn't loved.

Not even by my mom.

And so I came out wrong.

And he shouted this over and over till I believed it too!

Then I came to my senses.

Teach, in the end, I'd of been better off defending myself.

Cause, I swear to you in writing, at our home, there wasn't money, there wasn't nothing to eat, there wasn't even water cause it was black coming out of the faucet so you couldn't even wash.

But there was always love!

The lawyer should of said it.

Should of said the one thing saving my family was love, even if we were shit at all the rest.

But maybe, if the lawyer said it, I'd of got a worse sentence?

Well, I don't give a fuck, cause it's the truth.

And nobody can tell lies about the truth.

NOVEMBER 7, 1991, AND A THURSDAY THING

In here we get pizza once a week that's delivered from the outside and we lose our minds over it we're so happy!

It's a Thursday thing, like today.

We're all super happy from morning on, cause we're thinking we get to eat something good instead of just the crap they serve in the mess hall.

In here, they won't even let you have chocolate.

Teach, since you're decent, you sneak it to us sometimes, but if you want to cut this part so you don't get in trouble with the Warden, go right ahead, you don't need my permission.

Thursdays, the happiest of all of us is Marietto.

Marietto, he ain't dead but he's on his way: he's super skinny, got hardly a tooth in his head, and them he does are black. He's ghost ugly, scary ugly.

Marietto looks like shit.

When he was young, they found him in the middle of the road, like a dog. He lived in a church, then he escaped, and started living like the gypsies.

So Marietto's an orphan, but he don't give a shit. He's used to it—that's his life.

Only thing he's sorry about is he don't look like nobody he knows and it's useful looking like somebody.

To get by, Marietto stole at street markets and stores: chips, fruit, potatoes, peppers, bread, eggs, sometimes packs of cigarettes cause he likes to smoke and what kind of a life does he have without?

A life of shit!

They caught him when he was stealing stuff to eat inside a supermarket, in Margellina.

The judges didn't care and sentenced him.

But Marietto was just too hungry. What's he supposed to do? Die?

They can go die themselves!

Marietto's the only one in here who don't want to get out, ever, cause at least in here there's a place to sleep and food to eat, even if it sucks. Us in Nisida, we got: breakfast, morning break, lunch, break again, and dinner.

And for Marietto, who never got to eat on the outside, it don't seem real, and he's always saying: "You get to stuff your face in here! They treat you good!"

But that ain't true.

They treat us like animals, it's just that Marietto was worse off before and so for him it's better and Nisida seems like a five-star hotel.

Me, I'd of never put him in jail, cause he done what he done out of hunger and thirst and trying to stay alive.

But them judges, they judge on a full stomach.

Me, I'd make sure them judges didn't eat for a whole month before putting Marietto on trial.

Teach, you're always telling me "society don't want any deviation," even juvenile, and so it'll put little kids in jail that ain't done nothing wrong, they're only hungry and thirsty.

You're always talking about this "deviation," you say it's important for society to see the things that go on inside Nisida and also inside our heads.

So I get it. The society you're talking about is something out there, off the island.

And it'll never set foot in here and try to see us for who we are.

So introduce me to this "society," Teach, so I can learn it some manners. And about real life.

Me, I spit in society's face for saying it don't understand us.

Cause that ain't true.

It understands us just fine—it ain't like we're speaking Arabic or Chinese. Society speaks Neapolitan too, just like us. It just does it hidden.

But you, Teach, you set foot inside Nisida.

You ain't "society."

You're way better.

So I'm writing it down here, that prison's a total *munnezza*, so everybody outside will know.

But even if it's total crap in here, Marietto's still happy.

He says as soon as he gets out, he'll steal something quick, cause things are good on the island, you get to eat and sleep where it's warm.

I feel sorry for him, you know, and I always give him extra pizza on Thursdays. He always seems hungry, even when he's eating.

No one better see me give it to him, though.

And he knows it.

Word can't get around I feel sorry for Marietto—I'd lose my position and my pride.

In here they're afraid of me, cause I done good in the past and I killed somebody, so now they all think I can kill whoever I want. Even in here. And that I got no pity.

Me, if I had a gun, there's a reason.

And it's good they're scared of me.

If I could, I'd shoot em all in the face.

Crack their heads open, cause I'm bad, real bad.

Torture em, make em scream.

Break their legs, break their fingers and toes.

Cept Marietto and Corrado.

And you, Teach.

And Franco, him never.

And not that guy in the mess hall. Cause he always gives us extra when we're hungry.

The other day was Sunday and Don Vicienzo came calling to say Mass in his tunic and his little scarf.

He's the prison priest.

Don Vicienzo's got a church in Chiaia, a nice place. So he's not exactly thrilled coming here, cause in Chiaia people don't sin too bad so he don't have to work too hard.

He don't feel like working hard. He's ugly and old, but not just now—that guy was born old. He's a real zero, even if he is a priest.

Don Vicienzo hates everybody in here.

The first one the priest couldn't stand is Abdu, who's illegal, was born illegal, so he's got no hope really. He's sixteen.

But Teach, you said we got to be especially kind to Abdu, more than anybody else.

Those like him, they made a "journey." They come to Italy hidden in trucks carrying gasoline, and they come to find happiness. But then they get in with the wrong people, start using, spit all over the place, pick fights, and die poor.

So much for happiness!

Don Vicienzo's got him by the balls cause Abdu don't speak our language. The priest thinks God just talks Italian, but everybody knows that ain't true cause if it was he wouldn't be God, just some guy like you and me. Maybe more like you.

And it ain't cause Don Vicienzo's a racist. He hates the whites in here too.

Actually, he hates me most of all.

He's always saying I'm the worst one in here, cause I didn't just murder a guy, I'm also the son of a whore and everybody knows it—I got it written all over my face.

To him being a whore's way worse than killing people.

He's always saying he won't have a woman like that in his church. He can recognize one blocks away, like he's got a hooker radar.

Well, I'll tell you: my mom always goes to Mass and the priest of the chapel by us, in Forcella, is a good person, cause he don't give a fuck how somebody earns. His church is near our *vicolo*, between two buildings that are falling down, and if you didn't know it was a house of God, you'd just think somebody lived there.

Mom had me baptized too, and I take communion. But I wasn't confirmed, cause I didn't have the time.

It don't matter to Don Vicienzo that I was baptized. I got no right to the sacraments—that'd be a very mortal sin.

He thinks if someone's real bad, he can't change, not even if he takes a shower in holy water.

Anyway, at Mass last Sunday—that ain't real Mass cause

42

we ain't in church, we're in jail—Don Vicienzo kept on sermoning: that's when you think the Mass is over but the priest just keeps talking and don't shut up.

And Don Vicienzo was talking talking, the old windbag.

We were all dying.

Even the Warden fell asleep.

But Don Vicienzo didn't notice nothing. When that guy talks, it's like he's on something, like he's possessed.

Talks in Italian, Latin, and other languages all mixed together.

Anyway, during his sermoning, Don Vicienzo said God created us in his image and likeness, and Marietto was super happy, cause at least he looked like somebody.

Then the priest said the end of the year was coming, but you don't need some saint to know that, just look at a calendar.

Then he starts screaming: "Repent your sins! Ask for forgiveness to find your way back to the right path, because now you're all twisted!"

Then he said that to straighten out we have to forgive those who hurt us.

And that's a direct order from God.

Whatever—I don't take orders from nobody.

Specially not God. He can do anything he wants and no one's got the guts to tell him off.

Cause people are scared he'll get even.

Not me.

I'm brave enough to look God in the eye and tell him what I think!

Not now though.

Some other time.

Don Vicienzo also said Our Lord loves us even if we're stinking bastards, that he created us without asking nothing in return.

So you think I need to thank him? God, he created me so bad, he must of been pissed off that day.

You know what I think: it's my mom who created me more than God. Plus my dad some. That bastard. Less him.

Actually, yesterday was his birthday.

I remember the date, how old he is, no—he's been in jail too many times. My father, when I saw him last, he was maybe thirty, maybe older. He ain't like other fathers. You think they're all alike, like moms. But fathers, they're all different.

I don't know when mine's getting out, but I know it'll be after me. And when he does, no way I'm going looking for him, cause I ain't no bitch.

My dad, he was trouble.

He drank and took a bunch of drugs and I don't mean sleeping pills. I mean the kind that keep you up, that make you violent.

He didn't listen, didn't talk, and if he did talk, it was just to swear.

When he went to work, we didn't know if he'd turn up live or dead, free or in jail.

Either way, Mom was always scared.

I remember.

He kicked the shit out of her, beat her so much, she could hardly walk.

Dad's been to jail a whole bunch in his life, but never for all the beatings he gave my mom. And I never understood that. Them's crimes too, but no one punished him.

When he came home, me and Vittoria, we hid in the bathroom. She plugged her ears so she wouldn't hear Mom scream.

Not me.

I wanted to remember it, my mom screaming.

When my father came home, Mom'd cross herself a lot and kiss her statue of Santa Rita that she kept over the stove. But Santa Rita didn't give a fuck, she had other shit to worry about, and my father, soon as he walked through the door, he always started beating on her.

The next day, Mom'd be covered in bruises.

But she pretended like she didn't see them, like they were normal.

But that ain't normal!

And then there's all of you, in here, saying I need to forgive my father anyway.

That I need to forget everything he done to us, cause then I can move forward stead of backward.

But you gotta have the stomach for it!

And then, for my mom, how can I forgive him for her?

Anyway, yesterday was his birthday, so I better quit thinking about it and write that letter like I promised you, Teach, and the social worker too.

Can you send it then? Cause I ain't got the revenue stamp.

But do letters reach Bergamo from the South?

Dear Dad, you bastard,

Some things need to be said and wrote down.

How are you?

Like you know, cause of course you know, I'm in jail, same as you.

But I'm a bit better than you, and you know this too.

Yesterday was your birthday and today I am writing you a letter to say happy birthday.

But only cause they made me, if it was up to me I'd of just wrote you swear words. But Mrs Martina corrects me, she's the teacher and she treats us good, and it's good she's here.

This place is a shithole, everything sucks, the prison stinks like sewer, me most of all, cause I've lived here plenty long and we don't get to shower when we want.

The island's isolated cause that's how God made it, but I'd of liked it a little less isolated.

But you know this too.

You know everything!

But, really, you don't know jack, do you?

Vittoria got married and she don't talk to us no more.

She's already got kids. I'm an uncle and you're a grandpa, like you give a shit.

Mom, I haven't seen since I been in here.

But I still love her, cause love ain't something you got to see.

I got furlough at Christmas and go home for two days almost.

If you want I'll tell her hello for you but I know you don't want me to, cause you're a bastard.

But I'm doing it anyway, and it's sure to make her happy.

And I'll kiss her on the forehead. That'll get her.

Dear Dad, I don't know what else to say, I already went to town here.

So I promised to forgive you for everything, even though you don't give a shit about nothing.

So: I forgive you.

But I hope you have to take at least one huge dump every month for what you done.

Dear Dad, take it easy.

Your son,
Zeno

My mom's beautiful. Like you, Teach. But she's different beautiful, cause she's my mom.

When I see her, I'm not a man, I'm just a son.

But God Almighty only gave her one face. You can never really tell if she's happy or sad. But you, Teach, you got a thousand faces—it's in your eyes. So you can tell when you're feeling good, or when you're dying inside.

Not my mom.

She's always got the same face on.

I ain't never seen her cry. Or laugh neither.

I'd like at least one time to see her do both—not together. One then the other.

When I was out, my mom was always scared they'd kill me. She's real scared about dying, but not in general. About *me* dying.

She always said a child dying ain't natural and that she had to go first, or my bastard dad before anybody.

When I went to jail, Mom was happy.

The last time we spoke, she said the sound of jail doors closing was better than the sound of funeral bells.

So, when she found out the cops put me in jail, she was happy, like Corradino's mom, cause then they couldn't kill me no more.

In my mom's head, prison made me immortal. To her, I can't die no more, not even from getting sick. Let's hope no one tells her that's crap, so she can stay happy forever.

So anyway, now that I'm inside, she ain't afraid no more, she's calmer.

So maybe I need to thank the juvenile court cause my mom ain't so worried?

No, I spit on every one of them, all the courts in the world!

So Mom, the last time I actually saw her was at my trial, then never again. I don't know when she kissed me last.

I don't even dream about her now, but I sure do remember her.

She came to the hearings, every single day.

And she always had on the same dress, and I never want to forget it.

A pink dress, so pink everybody looked at her.

She was so beautiful, like when she was young, like before she became a whore.

But you could tell she felt like it was her fault, even if she was wearing pink and even if she never said.

She helped me with my business.

She filled the baggies I sold in the *vicoli*, so I could earn. When I went out, she stroked my cheek and told me may the *Maronna* go with me. But I always went out alone, cause truth is, that's just something to say and it was my responsibility and nobody else's.

My prices were good and my stuff was super high quality.

So they wanted to shoot me, cause I was some real competition for the others and I was stealing their areas and their customers.

So they had to get rid of me.

I never got caught by the police when I was working.

And yeah I know, Teach, you tell me not to brag about this stuff. But I can't help it. Cause it's no small thing. I was always having to run and no one ever caught me! I was super fast.

Mom couldn't tell me not to, cause I was doing what I had to.

Without me, we couldn't eat. We couldn't just live on what she did. So she kept quiet and helped me.

I don't know if she feels guilty for what happened, I mean for the guy I killed, who was young.

He was a son too. Like me.

Mom didn't ever talk to me at the trial, and we couldn't even hug.

I don't know if she feels guilty about me too. That I'm in here.

You, if you see her, tell her she don't have to feel guilty.

Not about nothin.

I'm actually glad they put us in school, in here.

But when I started, I didn't much like the idea of it, cause I was already in jail. School was another prison.

Then they told us they'd give us five thousand lire every day we come here.

And that ain't nothing to sneeze at!

Specially in jail: we can buy ourselves cigarettes, stamps, and other stuff I can't talk about, cause no one knows about it and I shouldn't either, but I do.

So going to school, we take turns, cause seeing how you pay us, everybody wants to.

Sometimes to go, it takes hitting somebody, but that's for the money.

One time I had to punch that scumbag Gennaro in the face: he thinks he's a boss in here cause he's got a beard, but that's just hair. I punched him and he crapped himself and let me go instead of him. So I got five thousand lire more.

I know you don't like that sort of thing, Teach, and you're always saying you don't want me to even say it.

But I gotta tell the truth, cause I promised you I would when I started writing.

So this is it.

In the beginning, I thought school really sucked. Nothing personal!

You're a woman, not school.

Then, time kept on, and I liked it.

Not all of it.

A little of it.

You teachers put us in desks around your chair.

Behind there's always two *surveglianti* watching us, cause we're kind of assholes and they don't trust us. You neither maybe!

In here, even school's a prisoner.

There's a whole bunch of teachers in here, you know.

And we don't like them all.

Just you and maybe a couple others, but that's normal. We can't like them all, specially in our condition.

You teach us Italian and writers. Even poetry, but we don't understand much of that, cause poets talk funny.

Then there's Miss Katia who learns us numbers and math.

She's a beautiful woman, but she decided to be a math teacher anyway. Totore always looks at her sexual. But not in a normal way, he looks at her bad. It makes me sick to my stomach and one of these days I'm going to beat the shit out of that *zuzzus'*.

Mrs Mariella, she's also a good person.

She don't got no problems with Totore, nothing to worry about. We call her Mrs Fatty, but never to her face, that would hurt her. She learns us science, animals (like dogs, but also beetles, monkeys, humans). She learns us how we're made, inside and out: the organs, like the lungs, the heart—but the real heart—the spleen that hurts when we run or else when somebody kicks us, and all the stuff for peeing and eating, not all of it together though—gross!

Then there's Mr Paolo who I think is a fag, and I know you think so too, but if you can't say it, Teach, don't worry, he'll still be a fag anyway. And I don't got nothing against fags. Far as I'm concerned, they're men like me and any other, only they like things that if Don Vicienzo heard it, he'd make sure they burned.

Mr Paolo learns us just physical education, I mean gymnastics. But we love Mr Paolo anyway, cause he helps us out and lets us play ball and we get some fresh air.

Then there's Don Vicienzo and the penguin who learn us religion. But only their religion, nobody else's.

The best one in here, at school stuff, is Gaetano.

He's that handsome, blond kid who's got this hair curling on his forehead, like models on TV and home-shopping channels.

He's always in the desk up front and he never gets sick of school, even when the teachers are sick of it.

Gaetano's in here for murder too, but we call him "Gaetano the Innocent."

He killed a guy, but not really.

I mean, it ain't his murder.

Gaetano never killed nobody. He took the blame cause the real murderer was twenty-six, and if they caught him, he'd of got a minimum of life.

But not Gaetano, cause he's only sixteen and the judges got a conscience when it comes to ruining us little kids' lives.

So that guy, the real killer, he's the son of this asshole from the Health Department who promised to pay Gaetano's family a million lire every year Gaetano gets for taking the blame.

Gaetano's family, they're poorer than me and my mom put together, so they say yes.

Course they do!

I'd of done the same!

Gaetano got thirteen years and he's going to Poggioreale soon, cause he'll be legal. And he's scared. You're better off dead than going there. Gaetano ain't bad. He really likes studying, and he ain't so good at being in prison. He's top of our class.

Corradino ain't bad at school either.

Marietto's a dumbshit who don't even know how to talk.

Me, I'm okay, depending on if I'm messing around or if I feel like it.

I went to real school, you know. I mean, on the outside.

And I gotta say it was way worse than this in here.

I went when I was *piccirillo*.

Not a school in Forcella, past there. I don't remember where.

It was poor, poorer even than the kids that went there.

It was called "compulsory school," cause otherwise, why would we fucking go. But practically all of us quit and got into the business.

That school sucked, it was like the teachers thought they were doing us a favor, teaching there.

You ask me, they could of all just stayed home!

Every one of them was a big pain in the ass.

They looked us up and down and made us feel even worser than we were.

And it's not like them teachers came from Milan! Not even from Naples. They're small-town!

And they felt they were better'n us who come from Naples, even if it is only Forcella.

They treated us like animals and didn't give a shit if we studied or we didn't.

They weren't like you, Teach. And they even got paid more than you. They didn't give a damn if we weren't in class cause we were out stealing. Just so long as we didn't get into *their* pockets. And the more we weren't at school, the happier they were, cause they worked less.

They were all temps, cause the real teachers were hiding out and didn't want to come learn us, cause we were less than trash.

I didn't know how to read, then I learned, though I read real slow, like I'm blind.

Writing, you know I pretty much suck at, but you always correct me and so I'm learning little by little.

I'm the first in my family to know how to read and write.

Numbers, them I don't like and don't get. You know what I think? I think they could try to make themselves better understood and instead they just stay numbers and always want to be right.

Science I like, but only when it explains what we're like inside—outside, I don't give a shit.

And Italian, well, that's you being patient. In lessons, you tell us about writers' novels, "to open our minds," you say, like they're keys to our heads.

You read us stories and show us how good they're written. Cause you know we won't read no books on our own.

You say that this way "we'll mold ourselves," and we'll forget the crimes we done outside.

I can't say if that's true or if you're just telling yourself lies.

Our crimes, we'll always remember them, cause it's our life and we can't erase it.

Another time you asked me if I ever thought of some legal job I could maybe do when I get out.

Some job that ain't criminal.

A real job, like delivering mail or working at a UPIM store.

So I thought about it, I really did.

And maybe I want to become a writer of them novels you read to us.

Does that take studying?

Or can I become a writer like this, killing somebody and being in jail?

And what if I do become a writer? Who gives me money for that? Is there someone who pays me?

Writers, far as I can tell, are loaded, aren't they?

If they get paid by the word, they must be super rich.

Like that guy who wrote the novel about the *pover'omm'* with my name who's always smoking, the one you like.

Is he still alive? If he is, I want to meet him and ask how much he makes.

You're always saying we need to find a passion, that we need to "reform."

And that this can only happen with dreams and passions.

But then you also say we can't reform ourselves on our own, that you have to reform us.

And yeah, sure, I agree.

But before reforming us, could you maybe learn us a new life: the one out there?

I don't know how to make a new life, all I know is the old one.

And thank God I wasn't born no girl, cause all I'd know then is how to be a whore, like my mom.

Try to learn me a new life and I swear on all the dead souls in my family, I swear I'll become a writer!

There. I wrote it down, so now it's a promise.

A real writer, with money and paper and a pen.

But only if it pays good by the word, Teach.

Cause I don't want to be no hungry artist.

Better off just dying for real.

Yesterday I remembered the name of that guy I killed and I had to write it down, so I won't forget it again.

His name was Michele.

Like the archangel.

But he was a devil!

I went and told the penguin, not to respect this Michele: more cause I want my own soul to rest. I been told if I know the name of the guy I killed, then maybe there's still a little hope for me in Paradise.

But you know what that penguin said to me?

She said: I won't be spared from Hell just cause I remembered his name! That I was going there no matter what, cause I was damned at birth and the truth always comes out.

Well, excuse me, but why should I remember his name then?

But Teach, you said it was important to remember, cause he was just a kid like me who also got "off-track."

I know it, I know Michele was young like me. And no

doubt there's a tie that can't be broke between him and me, even if we don't know it.

Cause I killed him.

But, like I told you, he was getting ready to pull a gun on me before I did.

And if he did, the one writing you today would be him instead of me.

And I'm a whole lot nicer, believe me, it's the truth.

Not him.

Michele, I don't remember what he looked like, I just remember his job. They ordered him to kill me, and others after me.

Carmine, who's been here longer than me, said he knew Michele a little. They did their catechism together, up there in Sanità. And their fathers knew each other a bit too.

Carmine, he said this Michele wasn't so bad, but he had to shoot people, cause he had a mom sick with something no one knows about, but it exists. And it kills everybody. I don't remember what it's called.

There wasn't a doctor in Naples who could make her better, cause all the idiot doctors they saw didn't give a shit if Michele's mom was sick or dying.

So he wanted to take her to America and have real doctors work on her.

He could make a ton of money from the "assignments" they gave him. They were "blood assignments," and they paid real good.

The ones out there giving us the hard jobs, they know it's important to have kids who kill instead of them.

Michele, they told him to "kill that guy and then this one!" and then they'd pay him, just like a salary.

But you know how many people you gotta kill to go to America?

That's super far away, across oceans, seas, and deserts! So to pay for a trip like that, Michele had to make a whole catatomb of dead!

So, I was on the list.

I was the first guy he had to kill.

His first job.

And it didn't go too good, cause I heard his scooter come up beside me in the *vicolo*.

I'm not sure why, but I knew right away.

He didn't even have time to get off his scooter. He put his hand in his pocket, and I pulled out my pistol.

And fired.

Three times.

Cause I wanted to be sure.

So Michele didn't get to save even one lira for his mom.

He croaked right there on the street.

But it's not like I could let myself get killed so he could save up! I got a mom too and she might not be sick but she has to whore.

I need to think about her.

And I need to think about my Natalina, my girl, who I'll marry when I get out, cause she's waiting for me.

I don't know if Michele had a girl too.

Maybe.

He definitely had a mom.

So I'm a little sorry, when I think about her.
But it ain't on me we had to kill each other.
And it ain't on him.
It's on other people, and we can never say who.

NOVEMBER 12, 1991

Today I want to talk about my *'nnammurata*, the girl I love.

I got her out there.

Her name's Natalina Marrazzo.

She's a year and a half older than me, but what do I care, she ain't old, and me neither.

She lives on our *vicolo*, in Forcella, and we've known each other since we were *piccirilli*. I remember her when I was five years old, even four.

Natalina has dark hair like mine, and hers is long, down to here.

She's a little cross-eyed and her nose is a potato.

She ain't pretty and she's got a lisp. It takes a bit to understand her.

But I love her all the same, like people do when they been married a long time.

And I want to marry her.

Not now though!

I'm too young, and all I got is jail right now.

So let's hope Natalina waits for me.

I'll give her a wedding better than a queen's. We'll eat so much, and have the ceremony in a church, and I can already see my Natalina, dressed in white, with lace and the most beautiful veil that'd make even the *Maronna* jealous.

You'll be invited, Teach, you and your husband and daughter, and Franco the guard, and some of the bastards from Nisida, if they're out too and still alive and kicking.

But first thing, I need to ask her father for her hand, cause her family's old-school, kind of stone-age.

Natalina's father is named Sabatino and he gets pretty worked up, all the time, morning till night, cause he ain't got a job.

Sabatino Marrazzo is *'nu brav' omm'*, a good man, one of the few I've known. When you see them, you know who they are, and you're never wrong.

He never wanted to be some piece of shit in Forcella — he's super stubborn.

So he's always unemployed.

And Natalina's family is bad off, cause there's nine kids and that's way too many, even if you're rich.

Only Rosario, the oldest, does criminal stuff like me, worser than me.

Sabatino used to hit him, beat him. To make him turn around.

It didn't work.

Rosario just fought back, he spit and punched, in front of everybody, cause he didn't respect his father.

And he kept on committing crimes.

He hid his gun and drugs under the bed.

And Sabatino's son was barely home, just to sleep and get up again. He never even gave the family any money from his crimes, cause his father would rather starve and didn't want nothing to do with Rosario and his punk friends.

And so Sabatino Marrazzo kept on being desperate and poor.

There's only people in the third world poorer than Sabatino Marrazzo and you want my opinion some of them are better off—they could take up a collection in Africa to help him out!

So I gave Natalina presents that her father couldn't, even if he was working.

One time, a real gold necklace I stole off a beautiful woman near Piazza Trieste e Trento. It's not like that woman needed it, and my Natalina did. I could of sold it, but I didn't want to, that necklace belonged on my *'nnammu-rata*, period.

I took her to eat *pizza a portafoglio*, at the Pignasecca Market, cause Sabatino didn't even have the money for that.

I took care of Natalina, and that's why Sabatino couldn't stand the sight of me, partly cause he was jealous, being her dad, and partly cause I was doing illegal stuff, like Rosario.

Me, I spit on unemployment.

Sabatino Marrazzo thought I was contagious, that my crimes would infect her, but it ain't a disease!

Still, Sabatino thought I'd make Natalina do criminal things, pickpocketing, holding. Or he thought I'd sell her on the streets, pimp her, like she was a real woman.

I'd never do that!

I never took her with me to commit crimes, and definitely not for her to be a whore, and if I wanted to, I had the right connections to make her one, and she'd be the best in all of Forcella.

Sabatino, like I been telling you, he really is a good person.

He did have normal jobs, but he wasn't good at nothing and always wound up fired.

He was a fruit vendor, a streetcleaner, did construction, once even cleaned toilets at Loreto Mare Hospital. He even worked in a coffee bar, though he was forty years old. And he never had enough money.

Everybody in the Camorra, they've offered Sabatino a ton of work, in Ferrovia too.

He won't even park cars illegal. He wants honest work, those things that don't earn and are pretty much useless, specially when you got nine kids!

But I'd of liked a father like Sabatino Marrazzo anyhow, stead of the one I got who's in Bergamo with a bunch of convictions.

I hope Sabatino Marrazzo becomes the richest man in the world someday and forgets about unemployment. Cause even if he disgusts me some, I love him.

I hope Sabatino Marrazzo gets to be so rich, even rich people bow down and kiss his feet!

And most of all, the State!

Sabatino was always fighting, him and the State, it was endless.

He wrote letters. Night and day. Then he went around Forcella saying: "I wrote this, I wrote that—to the goddamn State!"

But nobody listened to him cause Sabatino Marrazzo's too honest.

And the State never even wrote back.

Sabatino would go around saying the State had forgotten him and he'd be in the *vicoli* every night shouting: "I'll make em remember the name of Sabatino Marrazzo!"

So you know what he done?

He tried to kill himself with Rosario's pistol. In the middle of the night!

We were all asleep and he woke up the whole neighborhood when he shot himself.

But Sabatino was even bad at that, cause he was too scared to die. He missed his temple and hit his ear.

So now he can't hear too good neither!

Me and my mom, when we heard the gunshot, we thought they'd come to kill us, and we were scared to death.

But it was just Natalina's father wanting to make the State remember him.

And the State ain't never even heard of Sabatino Marrazzo—they don't know nothing about him!

But I know.

And now you know too.

Me and Natalina didn't do it, cause she was still too young and if her father found out, he'd of smashed both our teeth in.

But sometimes I'd take her out at night.

She'd leave without telling nobody. Besides, Sabatino drank to forget being poor and Natalina's mom was dead and couldn't say nothing.

I'd take her to Piazza Plebiscito, at three in the morning.

I'd come get her on my scooter, wait by the first floor of her building. And we'd ride down the middle of the *vicoli*. I'd go to Via Roma, then Piazza Trieste e Trento, then to Plebiscito.

You always see the piazza in the daytime, with all the cars, right?

You know it with all the noise, the traffic, all the people coming to buy nice things, expensive things, the bars with all the rich people eating and drinking right in front of us.

But the way I see it, at three in the morning with my Natalina, nobody else sees it.

Everybody's asleep, even the stone lions laying below the church.

The two of us, we'd walk holding hands, like grownups do when they're together.

Then we'd go back to being *piccirilli* and run all over the piazza, race each other to the church. We'd fall, even on our faces, but we never got hurt.

Then we'd go sit on the lion, the bigger one, though I guess they're both just about the same.

But our lion was always the one with the big eyes.

And me, I'd get on, and her behind me, and I'd pretend we were riding a horse.

One night I wrote on the lion's ass: "*Z. e N. pe' semp'*."

Teach, if you go by Plebiscito, could you maybe look at the lion's ass and see if what I put's still there?

It's the one on the right, when you come from Piazzetta Carolina.

But Natalina, like all respectable girls, played hard-to-get, like my mom told me about, and she wouldn't even give me one kiss!

I'd of liked at least one, but she was super stingy and made me suffer.

She'd say: "No! *Non simm' manc' spusat'*. My husband gets my kisses — not you!"

Then I'd trick her, cause I'm super good at that.

I'd say: "Natalì, *Maronna mia*! Getta a load of that! A shooting star, look how big, look at that big fat tail!"

And when she'd stare up where there wasn't nothing, and turn around to tell me to stop my teasing, it's then I'd pull her close.

I'd look her right in her cross-eyed eyes.

And kiss her.

And she'd pretend she was mad.

I'd hug her.

And she'd pretend she was mad again, but it wasn't true. She'd smile at me.

Then I'd touch her real soft.

And I never seen nobody do it before.

But I know how it's done.

Some things you don't make up — you're born knowing.

Anyway, Teach, them kisses, and touching my Natalina, they were the most beautiful things I ever stole.

I finally got Totore.

I told you it was only a matter of time—you just had to trust me.

We do fight in here sometimes, I mean there's kicking and punching and spitting. Slaps and head butts.

I know that's upsetting, Teach, but it shouldn't be. It's normal. We pound on each other so we'll feel less like we're in prison and more like we're out there, like we were before we got in here.

And we do worser too, but not that much worser. Cause we don't want to be up on other charges—hitting somebody's always a crime.

We swear too, say all kinds of awful things, but never curse God, cause that ain't right: he don't talk, so he can't fight back.

We only curse humans.

Anyway, the other week, I got that scumbag Totore.

He's a sick fuck, so it felt real good.

He's here for sexual assault.

That's an adult crime, not a kid crime!

The Warden says Totore is "precocious."

Precocious!

He's a total creep.

I got a mom and a sister, and I can't stomach that sort of thing. Women gotta be respected. When they want to be respected, that's what they get. If they say different then you don't gotta respect them, but only cause *they* want it!

So anyway, the other week, Totore said something totally *zozzo* to Miss Katia.

She's got these long long legs, skyscraper legs. But she's shy. You want my opinion, she has to come here, cause she's actually scared of us. She's scared shitless of all men, even boys, and that's why she's older and never been married.

So the other day, Miss Katia's wearing this skirt and she's explaining square roots.

And then Totore gets up from his desk and looks at her like he's a real man, like he's thirty, and she's just this beautiful woman.

And he says this sick fuck thing.

I can't even write it down, cause it's too embarrassing.

Something really sick! Like from a porno movie—even the guards in the classroom couldn't believe it!

Then Miss Katia, never married, even though she does got nice legs, she turns red like a sweet pepper and hides her face in her hands.

After his smut nasty talk, Totore runs out of the room, cause he knows he's in for it.

But the guards catch him and take him to the Warden, who should kill him but just writes up an incident report on him. A report don't mean squat to somebody like Totore—he don't give a shit. Even medicines don't stop him.

So I intervened.

I went out into the hall. And the guards were holding him, and I kicked him in the balls.

He screamed and cursed all the dead in my family.

Everybody else cheered me cause I was a hero.

I never been no hero before and it felt pretty good. I definitely recommend it.

I felt like Batman—Prison Batman!

But then that scum Costantino comes in. He grabs me from behind, turns me around and punches me twice in the face. My nose starts gushing blood.

So the Warden runs in, mad as hell. Screams we're all a bunch of bastards, that's all we are.

After he's done cursing us out, he calls the doctor.

That doctor comes running, cause the Warden pays him cash.

He's only in Nisida once a week, he's got his office in downtown Naples, in a building with balconies, and it's all legal.

When that doctor came in, he didn't say nothing.

He looked at me, a little disgusted. He treated my nose that was ugly to begin with and that ain't changed. But who cares—I don't plan on being no actor. The Warden thanked him and paid him, then he thanked God, but him he didn't pay even one lira.

Me, though, I got two days solitary confinement.

The Warden said if Totore wasn't such a punk he'd of had to call the police for me to stand trial again, and it would of been worser than before.

But I don't care.

It was worth it!

That's why I wasn't in class the other day, Teach, I wanted to tell you here.

The Warden told me I almost lost my Christmas furlough. But I told him what I done was called for, that Totore got what he deserved, and none of us wanted him in Nisida no more, cause he was a filthy turd.

And you know what happened?

To avoid more trouble, they sent Totore to Santa Maria Capua Vetere!

While I'm still stuck here, by the sea!

Does that sound right to you?

Does it?

Well, at least we don't have to see that bastard's face no more, and we can all relax.

Miss Katia can wear skirts again, no problem, cause we're polite and we keep our mouths shut and only look at nice legs and maybe dream about them at night, cause we're still men, after all.

But don't tell her!

She's super touchy now and might report us for our dreams. And they ain't dirty anyway. They're love dreams!

My lawyer told me we can't be punished for what's in our heads.

And that's where our dreams are.
They just can't come out.
That's right, ain't it? Cause if not, it's a real problem.
Even for those not in jail.

Yesterday, Gaetano the Innocent killed himself.

I saw him.

He was there, lying on a stretcher, like he'd been dead forever, like he died natural.

He was still handsome with that hair curling on his forehead, the way he was before he died.

He hung himself with his sheet in his cell.

His bunkies didn't hear. He died silent, not asking nobody for help cause he didn't want none. Everybody was asleep.

In here they take all our things, so we don't cut ourselves, kill ourselves, slit our throats. But sheets and blankets they don't deny nobody, cause it's damp on the island, specially in winter.

So it's the one thing we got, if we've been tired forever and want to die.

Franco came. He put his hands in his hair and cried. Then he kissed the rosary he keeps close, and cried some more.

He was losing it, cause he kept telling everybody, "I could of stopped it."

But how?

For me it was super strange seeing a man cry, more than seeing a man dead.

I never seen it in person, it's the kind of thing you see on TV. But here was Franco crying like a baby, and not even ashamed.

My mom always told me there was men who cry, not just women. But I just thought it was something she said. Dad, for instance, he never cried, Mom says so too.

I wasn't close to Gaetano—he seemed too handsome, too smart. I felt like an idiot around him.

But I was sorry he killed himself, cause it could of happened to any of us, including me.

Corradino was mad.

Gaetano made him remember his mom. They didn't have nothing in common, but both of them were dead and that was enough. So for the first time, yesterday Corradino didn't talk with the spirits, he was too pissed off.

You ask me, Gaetano deserved being "reformed" more than everybody else in here.

He was always doing his homework. He never hurt another living soul. He always paid attention and never looked at nobody's legs.

You ask me, Gaetano could of done great things!

He could of become President, or a prison warden, or run a post office or a hospital. Could of run something, anyway, cause he had a good head on his shoulders.

Gaetano could of become an actor, cause he was handsome.

Or a model, with money coming out of his ears.

But instead, he just became dead.

Dead by suicide.

And now that he's dead, you ask me, that guy in the Health Department won't pay his family no more, I'm sure about that. So in the end he went to jail for nothing.

Gaetano was a good kid, but next week he would of been legal and he was scared shitless to go to Poggioreale.

I'll be going there too, but in two and a half years. But I don't want to be scared there—if I am, I might kill myself too, but that'd really hurt my mom, cause she thinks I'm immortal.

This morning, Don Vicienzo held a kind of Mass in Gaetano's honor, though it's never a real Mass, we only pretend like it is.

They can't hold funerals in here. But Gaetano's gotta be let out somehow, at least now that he's dead.

During his sermoning, Don Vicienzo didn't say nothing about Gaetano not really being a murderer, cause he didn't give a shit. *Chill' 'o prevet' sape tutt' cos'!*—the priest knew all about it! But he pretended he didn't know nothing, just like a *Camorrista*.

And he also said he don't know if Gaetano can go to Heaven, on account of what he done.

God, he don't want to see nobody who committed suicide or murder.

Don Vicienzo said God don't give a shit about them people, and he'll send them flying down below with a good kick in the ass, to go and be in the fire with the devils.

That priest wants to scare us.

He wants us to be terrified of God, to be scared shitless when our time comes. He says it partly to make us repent the things we done and partly cause he's a bad person.

Then, at the end, Don Vicienzo said something beautiful. He said you don't get any older when you die.

And this I liked.

Cause now that Gaetano's dead, he can stay young forever. And can stop being scared of Poggioreale.

No more birthdays for him. No more years, months, minutes, hours.

And then I prayed I just keep getting older forever, and don't never stop.

Sunday night I got a good look at the sea.

Marietto came too, cause the sea makes him think of fish-fry.

Teach, I know you're crazy about the sea, not just cause of fish-fry—you're always talking about it.

You tell us we're lucky being above it, here at Nisida.

That it's much better here than Santa Maria Capua Vetere and you're sorry when we ask for a transfer.

So Sunday I looked out the window.

And there was the sea.

Outside, like always—course it's never inside, that ain't its nature.

And the sea wants to be looked at, cause it's full of itself.

The sea gives me a big pain in the ass, sorry, Teach, but it's true.

Anyway, I followed your advice.

You told us there's poetry in its water and that we're lucky to be so close. That we have to see this poetry and use our imaginations a little more.

You gave us an assignment in class: "Find something beautiful in the sea and tell me about it: what does the sea make you feel?"

Nothing.

It bugs me.

Its water is salty and you can't drink it!

What's the point of water if you can't drink it?

It's got useless water.

Then it, I mean the sea, is infinite.

That's what you said and I didn't really want to know it was infinite, cause now it bugs me even more, if that's even possible!

The sea's got the rizen, and you told me it's called the "horizon" and thank you for correcting me, cause I learn things better that way.

This horizon is also infinite.

So Marietto asked me what that means.

And I said if something's infinite, it can't be put in jail. It's always free.

And that's enough to make the sea suck.

Marietto said he thought so too, that he spit in the sea's face, cause it ain't fair.

But that we can't do, cause it ain't got a face or eyes.

Who does the sea think it is, anyway—it's just useless water.

And you want me to tell the judge who sentenced me: "Dear judge who sentenced me, and all you other judges, you pieces of shit. You sentenced me to a whole bunch of years in jail, and that was right, cause I killed somebody.

But why'd you have to put me by the sea?

Did you know it was infinite, or didn't nobody tell you?

I don't know if you realize, but I'm totally finished.

Dear judge or judges who sentenced me, you could of put me in a jail on a street that's never infinite cause there's stoplights.

A prison where I might look out the window and see people worse off than me, like Africans or gypsies asking for handouts.

But, no, you put me by the sea and here's what I see out the window:

Boats.

Yots that are boats but rich ones.

People having fun, like we ain't there but we are.

Rafts and floaty rings.

And beach umbrellas.

I see all the things I could never have, even if I was free.

My mom could never take us to the beach, cause she was busy, you understand?

Dear judge or judges who put me in jail, this don't seem fair to me, but what do you think?"

But it's not like they'd answer me anyway, cause they got plenty else on their plates and they're sentencing other juvies, worser than they sentenced me.

Anyway. The other day, I got a note, here in jail.

A note from the outside.

Brung by someone new in here, from my neighborhood, named Peppiniello 'o scem', who sells black market cigarettes.

In this note, I don't know who wrote it, it said that I gotta die.

That's what it said: I gotta die.

But in Neapolitan.

I'm not too worried, cause in the end we all gotta die, so it ain't exactly a surprise.

But Teach, you were worried—you ain't used to that sort of thing.

You called the Warden right away. You're a good woman, and you thought about the ugly things that might happen to me.

The Warden, afraid cause he was responsible and not for any other reason, asked the judge to send me to Forcella with Franco when I got my Christmas furlough, but also with a real policeman, armed and everything, so I'd get my own guard, just like the President of the Republic.

You understand? Like I'm somebody important!

So I'll get tons of respect! Specially in Forcella where no one important ever comes, or if they do, it ain't for long.

Let's hope I can get a photo with Franco on the outside at Christmastime—that would be a riot.

Franco is *n'omm' buono*, cause he ain't so rich and he's got a criminal for a dad. He's worried they'll hurt me too, but I told him it ain't the first time I been threatened, that it's normal in my line of work.

I promised him the first piece of *capitone fritto*.

I'm sure my mom'll make it for Christmas Eve, cause *capitone* is a tradition and we get it from the fish vendor by our place, and this guy's always fair and never tries to cheat nobody.

I sure do love *capitone*, Teach!

I dream about *capitone*! It's such a bummer we only get to eat *capitone* at Christmas, that it ain't allowed the rest of the year.

Do you know why that is? I don't.

Hey, do *capitoni* live in the sea, or in rivers?

I always wondered.

If they're in the sea, you think we could try to fish for them, maybe from our cell window?

At least that way, the shit sea can make itself useful.

Me, I begun in my profession cause of a guy in Forcella.

This "guy in Forcella" is named Ciro, but I won't say his last name.

He was a regular of my mom's, and that ain't nothing to be ashamed of, cause it's honest work.

Ciro comes from a big family, everybody knows them in Forcella, and sometimes in Soccavo too.

He needed a kid to run errands.

I was a kid, and then I grew up, but first I was a kid.

I've always been good on a scooter. I learned when I was ten! Never crashed one. Even when I was *piccirillo*. One time, though, I got pushed off, by some guys looking to beat me up. I fought back though. And I lost a tooth, one in the middle.

So Ciro needed a kid to make deliveries, bring his customers their supply, some of them living in rich, beautiful places in Posillipo.

Then he had me start working full time. Even got me a

gun for security. But he didn't learn me how to use it—like I already told you.

Ciro liked to razz me.

He'd say I was a chip off the old block, cause my dad was in jail and my mom did what she did, so I was born for this line of work.

He said I had a future ahead of me.

That I could be like him, or almost.

That I could get my mom off the streets and then get back at everybody who always thought we were trash.

Truth is, Ciro knew we needed this.

And so I begun.

But when I started delivering for him, and also selling baggies, I was scared.

Scared shitless.

I was only twelve, so I had a right to be, don't you think?

But I never told nobody, cause it would of been worser if I had. Ciro can't stand pussies, and I didn't want to lose my job or my pride.

I was afraid of the police, of jail, but most of all that Ciro's competitors would kill me.

Cause in the papers there was a bunch of people killed, and we knew who did it.

And I'd think that one morning it'd happen to me, that I'd show up in the *Mattino*, beaten to death.

I couldn't sleep at night.

I had insomnia, like real grownups.

I was scared they'd come and take me while I was sleeping and they'd also hurt my mom.

So I pretended to be asleep, or else Mom would of worried and I didn't want that. She already had enough troubles.

Maybe you think it's easy to pretend, but that ain't true! You can't just shut your eyes!

It's real work, you gotta concentrate.

I'd squeeze my eyes closed real tight, cause they had to stay shut. And to try and stay calm, I thought about being alone on a desert island.

But not a peaceful island. Ferocious lions lived there!

And I'd imagine not being scared of them, that I was super strong.

I had a bunch of knives and I was going to dominate the lions all on my own.

I hit them, kicked the shit out of them, tamed them.

And I came out alive in the end!

And I'd tell myself if I could kill imaginary lions on that island, I didn't have to be scared of nothing or nobody, not even them who could kill me down in the *vicoli*.

And at some point, I always fell asleep for real.

And when I woke up in the morning, I could get ready for work and not be worried, cause I got some rest.

My mom would be there and she'd make us coffee.

I drunk coffee since I was twelve.

Even in here, before I go to sleep at night, I think about *my* island instead of this island.

But not cause I'm scared, more cause I'm bored.

Teach, my island's so beautiful—if I could, I'd show you so you'd understand, cause my words don't do it justice.

And I can't draw it for you cause I don't know how.

If I did, you'd just make fun of me and tell me it sucks. So I'll write it down.

On my island, everywhere is sand, not rocks. With beaches so sugar white you'll want to eat them.

Right in the middle, there's my hut, not a hut though, a two-story villa, like a real *Cammorista* lives in.

No—forget the two floors—it's got infinite floors.

Every day, I call up this friend of mine who does construction work under the table. And one and two and three and a thousand and up I go, clear up to the sky!

And all around the villa, there's these ginormous terraces. But no windows, and no doors or roof.

It's gotta be all open and nothing can close. On my island, there's only exits, but you can come inside.

It's magic.

There's also a tram that leaves from behind the villa and takes me right inside the Stadium, where I have my own section behind the goal and I cheer for Naples, even if that *scornacchiato* Maradona left us.

I put flowers, red roses, all around my balconies, cause my mom likes red roses.

But not short ones, like they keep in cemeteries. My mom likes the ones with the super long, skinny stems, the kind of roses for those alive and kicking.

No one ever brings her flowers, not her customers, cause men who pay a woman turn to bastards and think money's a substitute for flowers, but it ain't.

Dad's in jail and can't give her none, but even if he could, the only thing he ever gave her was a beating.

And I'm in here.

But even if I was out there, I wouldn't never think to get her roses, cause I ain't got the time. Plus, our money's for more important stuff, like eating and paying the loan shark his rent.

And so, when I make my villa on the island, when I imagine my villa, I fill it with red roses I grew for my mom. And we don't have to do no more begging.

And there's a little guest house too, just for my mom.

And she won't have to work no more, she can retire, cause it's the right thing, and she needs to!

And from her guest house, she can look out and see all them that called her "whore," and weren't respectful, and she can show off.

Then, in my garden, I'll build cages for them lions I tamed when I was *piccirillo*. They got all droopy when they got beat, cause they were scared of me.

But Teach, now I ain't afraid of nothing.

I ain't never been droopy, not even when they shut me up in here.

And nobody beats me.

But sometimes I like to get a little droopy, and see what happens.

It helps me relax some.

The other week, all you teachers kept after us, saying the Pope was coming to Naples.

And we made ourselves real clear: we don't give a shit if the Pope comes to Naples. Only if he comes and plays for Naples, cause with him playing forward, we'll win a championship for sure.

And that pissed you guys off.

For ten days before his vacation to Naples, you really got after us about making all these little do-dads, like we're five years old.

But we're not five years old.

You kept on and on about us making ceramic crucifixes and holy water fonts in the prison workshop.

Like the Pope don't got enough of that crap already.

He's got a million of them things, and all in gold and silver.

Who gives a shit about some plaster crosses we make in here!

Didn't matter—you made us do it anyway.

You, Teach, were the most honest and kind about it of everybody, and asked us to write a letter to the Pope.

Something from the heart, you said, but also a little bit from our heads, so not just talking shit.

So I wrote my letter.

We put a package together of all the things we wrote, the drawings, and the crappy crucifixes. We gave them to Don Vicienzo and the penguin.

You know what I think? As soon as them things leave here, they're getting tossed in the trash, and the Pope'll never lay eyes on any of it.

But we pretended like he would.

Here's what I wrote to the Pope:

Dear Pope,

They really got after us, here in prison, and we had to write you a letter, but you're not Babbo Natale handing out gifts for Christmas and you don't have to grant us nothing and of course you got bigger fish to fry.

But them in here said we had to. And that you're better than Babbo Natale!

They said we could ask you anything we want, and you'll answer.

So I come up with some questions:

How come there ain't no female Pope and how come you don't marry?

Is it cause you think women are trouble?

Dear Pope, that depends on the woman.

I don't got much experience, but I got some. Definitely more than you, cause you're kind of behind.

There are some women who are worser than men, that's true. And there's some who are just nasty, real ballbreakers.

Sometimes my mom's a witch, but she ain't a bad person. She needs prayers too. More than anybody, really.

Mrs Martina who learns us Italian is a woman, but she ain't no ballbreaker. Well, maybe ask her husband, cause he'll know more than me.

Another woman I know is Natalina, la 'nnammurata mia, *and she ain't bad.*

You ask me, you find yourself a nice woman, someone who cooks and cleans, and maybe you can marry her too, and settle down and live peaceful.

Dear Pope,

I got other questions. But I don't know if you got the time to answer everybody and I don't want to bug you.

But why is there Mass? Ain't it enough for God if we pray for our own stuff at home?

Don't he trust us?

Well he shouldn't.

And:

Why do we got to eat the body of Christ if killing somebody's a sin?

Do Popes sin too or don't you got the right?

Are there young Popes, or is it a rule you got to be old and bent over?

Does the Devil exist or did you invent him to scare the priests?

Do you really talk to God, or do you dream it, cause you're kind of old?

And if you do talk together, ain't it really him who does the talking cause he wants to be the star, or can you get a word in?

That God, he thinks he knows everything.

You ask me, there's tons of things he don't know and only pretends to.

But when you talk, does he listen?

Or does he do the same like when people pray who ain't the Pope?

Me, I never talk to him cause I think he's got better things to do but mostly cause I got awe!

He's God. I'm just Zeno.

Another question now, here goes:

When we die, does Jesus put us on trial, or can we just relax?

I already had a trial and it didn't go so well. I'm in here for a serious crime and I won't say what, but I hope you don't know, cause if you do, you'll send me to Hell without ever meeting me and that ain't right, cause you need to at least shake my hand first.

The teachers told us, if you got the time, you might even come here to Nisida.

But if and when you do come, don't expect us to repent for the crimes we done just to impress you and any priests you bring along.

Me, for example, I ain't never repented, cause I don't know how.

In here, everybody's told us that you can forgive us, but they also told us that God ain't no ATM, and so we got to have patience for forgiveness and pray, pray, and pray some more!

Sorry, but what kind of forgiveness is that?

Fake!

No, you can keep it!

Us in here, we need real forgiveness, not lies!

But I don't want to get too worked up, cause you're the Pope and you got magic powers.

I wanted to tell you, though, that I don't know how to pray.

They never learned me.

So you pray for me.

Best wishes to you and your family,

Zeno Iaccarino

I forgot to write you something important:

The priest you put in Nisida is an asshole.

So, dear Pope, you need to fire him.

I didn't choose who I was born to—this ain't no super-market.

People are born by chance, and nobody decides nothing.

For example, Teach, you must of been born to honest people, but not billionaires.

Same with your husband.

Your daughter was born to you.

Me, I was born to a whore and my father.

Carmine's the son of losers. Carradino's the son of *Camorristi*. Peppiniell's got a dad who robs folks on the Fuorigrotta–Margellina tram. Gaetano, who's dead, was the son of a *pover'omm'*. Gennaro's the son of a piece of shit. Marietto don't belong to nobody.

I don't know if we can be any different from them, when we're grown.

You already told me maybe I can become a writer, but I don't know if I can, or if that's just stupid.

Cause I don't want to fool myself. I'd just feel bad.

Then you took me aside one day in class and told me if I really wanted to be a writer, I had to always write and never stop, and not just now, forever.

And that I got to write about my life.

All of it, even if it's ugly, that's okay.

So this thing about life in books and novels, it got me thinking.

You know what I think? Nobody's got such a big life that they can fill a whole book.

That famous Zeno, the one you like, did him and his life really exist or is there some bastard behind him making it all up?

Nobody made me up!

My mom made me, but she didn't think about it.

I came, and that's it.

August 3.

Mom made me at home, like homemade pasta, though she never knew how to make pasta, just babies.

I came unexpected, cause it was supposed to be after the summer, but maybe my mom messed up her dates.

I don't know if my father was in jail or out doing something. My sister Vittoria was still little and couldn't help.

So my mom got me out on her own, without no help, not even from God Almighty.

Mom told me when I came out, my head was like a *cocozza* squash. And I was ugly, a hairy little monkey. Then I got better over time. She loved me from the start, even if I wasn't no beauty. My mom always says kids ain't no art museum.

They baptized me in Forcella, when I still had my squash head, and I ain't never left, cept for some purse-snatching in Margellina and a little in Posillipo, and so on.

I'm fifteen years and four months old. I'd like to still be this exact, even when I get out of prison. Instead, time's just going to go by, and not warn nobody.

In here, we ain't all the same age.

Marietto, he don't quite know how old he is cause he don't know when he was born exactly. So the judges decided on an age for him at the trial, cause it's required.

But he was fine without one—who cares?

But in the end somebody has to give you an age, and so they made one up. They said: "You're fourteen and that's that." You ask me, Marietto's younger than fourteen, but that wasn't convenient for them judges.

Corradino, he don't like his age—he thinks it sucks. Being fifteen's too young for him. Useless. He wants to be grown so he can take on serious work when he gets out. Sometimes he wants to be fifty so he can understand everything better and be treated like a real man. Sometimes he even wants to be seventy, but you ask me, that's way too old, even for a grownup.

Anyway, my birthday, I never celebrate it, not for years and years, not when I was out, either.

I don't remember how!

Mom never made me a cake with candles on it, but that was cause she didn't have the money. She wanted to, though.

When I was *piccirillo*, she'd say, "Happy birthday," and give me a big kiss.

She always remembered the date.

So I'd know it was my birthday and not a day like any other. But outside our home nothing changed and the day was always the same.

When Mom started being a whore though, she stopped kissing me in the morning and I lost track of my birthdays.

The judges reminded me at my trial when I was born. But not to give me no present!

In Nisida, we don't celebrate birthdays cause the more you grow, the closer you get to adult prison, so there ain't a whole lot to celebrate. No, you're more likely to cry, pray, even to die, but not me: I'm doing just fine.

I only remember one of them, when I was still outside. Before killing Michele.

I remember my birthday cause of that one day.

I was with my Natalina, the night of August 2. I really wanted to be with her, more that night than any other.

I drove my scooter to her place, like I always did, at night, when her father was asleep.

I didn't realize my birthday was the next day, but Natalina knew, cause girls keep track of that stuff.

That time with her, I wanted to spend the whole night together, till the sun got bored of sleeping and woke up.

It was sticky hot out.

The gnats were biting our legs and arms.

We rode by the sea on Via Caracciolo, to catch a breeze.

I parked and we looked at all the garbage tossed in the water.

Then Natalina took hold of my face and looked me in the eyes and told me she loved me.

But just for that one night.

And she explained.

She said: "Just tonight and that's it! Cause your birthday's at midnight. Don't start thinking I love you tomorrow, cause it ain't true!"

That's when I remembered about my birthday the next day.

And that was the last time I celebrated my birthday, but also the first time.

And the most beautiful, cause my Natalina told me she loved me.

Even if it was for just one night.

There's somebody I know who's come to Nisida.

His name is Tonino 'o Bulldog and that's how ugly he is.

Tonino 'o Bulldog lives in Forcella, just two *vicoli* from us.

He wanted to play for a national soccer team when he was little, he wasn't born a criminal, he inherited it from his uncle. Then you get used to it.

We never knew each other in Forcella, cause we're not the same age and we never did nothing bad together. He's older, maybe seventeen.

Tonino 'o Bulldog got arrested for dealing drugs, but he was barely holding. I don't know what his sentence was, but not super long, I think.

I keep the hell away from him.

I don't want to know nothing about what's going on around home, cause I ain't there, so it don't count.

And if something happens that ain't supposed to, I don't have to know about it, cause no one comes to visit, or writes me.

I want to stay out of it.

Once in a while, though, Tonino 'o Bulldog watches me. Not in a bad way, just watches, is all.

But definitely on purpose.

Me, I'd like to smash his face in, cause I gotta be unwatched.

Corrado tells me to cool it.

That I'm thinking on it too much and need to stop. And if I don't talk to him, he won't talk to me. And it don't mean nothing if he just looks at me, cause we ain't got nothing to do with him, we just keep to ourselves.

But every time I see Tonino, I feel the blood rushing to my head.

To calm me down some, cause it was really pissing me off, Corradino read my cards.

I got: a four of swords, a three of cups, an eight 'e renar', and an upside-down Ciro Ferrara.

Corrado said the four of swords was a wife, cups was children, so that meant three, coin cards was money—you don't got to be a genius to figure that one out—and Ciro Ferrara was good luck, cause it was Ciro Ferrara, so good enough.

He said my future looked real promising.

I said I didn't give a shit.

With the past I got, the best thing I can do sure ain't gonna be the future.

Today we celebrate the *Maronna*.

Maybe it's her birthday, I don't know.

Anyway, people on the outside don't work today. I worked though, even on feast days. We were poor, and when it's like that you can't just stop cause a priest says so.

This morning, we did our prayer of thanksgiving, along with the penguin, to the *Maronna*. But I only pretended, cause I wanted to thank my mom and not somebody else's.

Plus I was tired, cause last night I slept uneasy.

I dreamed I was dead, just like the kid I killed. I was dead but there wasn't no blood, you can also croak nice and tidy.

And it really wasn't too bad.

I'd become a ghost!

So I was dead, but not that dead.

It was super cool, cause I could pass through walls and doors, and spit in everybody's faces, and I didn't have to answer to nobody. And so the first thing I done was go over to Costantino's place, and really laid into him, slapping him, kicking the shit out of him. And no one could jail me for it, cause I could just pass through doors. All the judges could do is shut it.

I was better than the infinite sea.

I don't know though if I'll die for real, I haven't decided.

I mean, I know everybody dies, and there ain't no choice—I ain't stupid!

But I'd like to at least be able to choose my time.

I only hope, when I die for real, that a whole bunch of people cry. Corradino said he definitely will. And if he dies first, I'll cry for him. If we kick it at the same time, I don't know how we'll arrange it. We'll see.

But after I dreamed being dead and a ghost, then I dreamed about a real black shadow.

You could touch it, so it wasn't a normal shadow. I stuck my hand in, and it was like gooey chocolate pudding.

And then, just like that, it swallowed me up, and I couldn't get away.

Then I woke up and let out this scream so loud all the maggots came running to my wing.

Right away I asked Corrado what my dream meant, cause he's psychic. But he just called me a "*strunz*" and rolled back over, cause it was four in the morning and he was tired. He said all this screaming of mine was getting traumatic.

So I just laid awake and worried.

Truth is, I always wake up kind of anxious.

So I talked to the psychologist in here.

You can go see him when you're sad or when you're too happy, cause being happy here in prison ain't normal!

This psychiatrist guy didn't tell me nothing.

He just wanted to give me drugs to make me go to sleep and then wake up. So he either didn't have the skill to cure me or there wasn't no cure.

But I ain't stupid. I never take drugs, even the legal ones they give you.

Cause they make you have drugged dreams.

I only took something once and I didn't like it cause it was fake.

There's two or three guys in here, and I won't say their names, cause you already know. These guys, they took drugs on the outside, just like adults, and one of them's a real junky—Saverio Esposito.

Saverio, when he arrived, they had to tie him up and give him something to put him out.

I don't even want to have tied-up dreams.

So I wonder: how do you dream normal, and not take any of this crap?

Teach, you told me that dreams save us more than any prayers.

If the priest or the penguin heard you, they'd report you to God and also to the Warden, and that sad-ass wouldn't even defend you.

Me, I've forgotten how to really dream.

You'll have to learn us again.

And we'll do it, I promise. And those who won't, well, I'll have to learn them how to respect you, whatever it takes.

We'll all sit in front of your desk, mouths zipped shut, and listen.

But learning us numbers?

You should tell Miss Katia that ain't really necessary. Numbers, we already know, with all the adding up we got in here, all the sentences and furloughs and probations. Numbers is the first thing we know and the last thing we forget.

You told me we can dream with our eyes open and we don't even have to take no drugs to do it.

So I tried it out, like you said, with my eyes open.

I saw the wall to my cell, all the graffiti. Some of it ours, but also from those who came before us: names, nicknames, a bunch of stupid shit.

My name was there too.

Then I saw a beetle big as my hand crawling up the wall.

And I watched that too.

And then I lost my gift for dreaming.

For me, what I miss most outside is just that, the outside.

And this outside is a bunch of stuff. Home, even if it's broken. Mom, even if she's a whore. Good fried food. Riding horseback on my scooter.

Outside is also my Natalina and her hands, her crossed eyes, her arms, legs, and mouth.

I don't miss any friends, cause they're all bastards in Forcella, a bunch of *sapunar'*.

Out on the *vicoli*, I didn't know nobody really, just faces, names, the jobs people done.

Cept one kid named Pasquale Maria. He was older by two years, but that didn't matter.

When we were *piccirilli*, we'd kick a ball around or play hide-and-seek, and we got along super well, cause him and me were different alike.

Pasquale Maria's mom gave him a girl's name cause it was the name of the *Maronna*. She wanted to fix things a little for her son, so he could be somebody.

But by age nine, Pasquale Maria was already parking cars illegal on Piazza Dante, cause he wasn't skilled at being somebody.

Then he met me and things got worse, cause I took him purse-snatching.

Pasquale Maria's mom cursed me out good and always blamed me for ruining her son's life. Maybe she was right.

Then when I really started in the profession with Ciro, me and Pasquale Maria didn't see each other around no more. His family moved someplace else, to get away.

Not that it mattered.

He wound up in Nisida before I did.

Others told me.

But I ain't seen him since I been in here. I looked for him in every group, checked out all the faces, one by one, and there ain't exactly a million of us.

Never found him though.

I miss him some, cause I think we were friends even though we didn't know it, and that kind of thing you don't forget.

I also asked Corradino what he missed from the outside. He said he didn't miss nothing, but I think he's lying. He misses everything.

Marietto misses the parents he don't know.

I couldn't say about the others, cause I ain't asked, and it's their own fucking business anyhow.

The truth is, Teach, we can't exactly say what we miss most about the outside.

You asked me if I miss committing crimes.

I don't miss my business, not that, but I do miss being somebody.

Now I'm nobody.

I'm just me, no big deal.

In Forcella, I was still always me, but people were scared of me too, cause I had good connections and a gun and also Ciro, whose last name was Varriale. There, now I told you.

He protected me, not cause he liked me. He was protecting his business.

I was his business.

Ciro didn't give a fuck about living or dying. Just being in charge and getting his money. That guy don't even care if he dies.

He's been in Poggioreale a bunch of times, but never for the real serious things we all know he done but nobody talks about.

Ciro's only been in jail for minor offenses, or when he's remanded to custody. Then he pays his top lawyers who're worser than him and they get him out and he's clean as a whistle.

And then he starts back up worser than before.

In the *vicoli*, everybody calls him *Cecato*, cause he stuck a pen in his eye when he was *piccirillo* to show he'd do any bullshit thing he wanted.

He's killed a bunch of people, but not cause he had to. It was also for fun.

When he picked me to work for him, I didn't have no choice.

My mom neither.

Once I started working for Ciro, he didn't pay my mom no more.

He got it for free.

Mom just wanted Ciro to protect me, and that's it. But in the end, I done my own protecting.

Ciro would come by our place about five, five thirty. I'd go out a bit before then, cause I didn't want to see him. I'd head out on my scooter.

When I got back, he'd be gone and Mom and me could get to work.

We'd prepare the baggies that evening or later that night.

Then we'd put them under the mattress or hide them in the toilet tank—in saran wrap.

Our place never got searched, and Ciro knew it. Mom had her other work that was out in the open. And that wasn't against the law, she was self-employed.

In the mornings, I went out and did my deliveries, after somebody told me where to go and when.

Problem is, Ciro got into it with somebody, a guy named Marcello, who wanted complete control of Forcella.

So wars broke out.

Like real wars, Teach, the kind you tell us about in school. Not with tanks, but only cause you can't get tanks down the *vicoli*. If you could, we would.

Sometimes, during the fighting, there'd be someone who'd wind up dead, or more than one, depending on the battle.

Definitely some pretty badly wounded.

I never wound up dead, but I come close.

And Ciro, after I killed Michele, forgot about me.

With my sentence, he couldn't use me no more. And he forgot about my mom too, that's for sure, but she's used to people forgetting about her.

Well, anyway, there's also decent people in the *vicoli*, not just the bad ones like me and Ciro. I need to write about them too, cause it's only right.

And the decent people don't harm nobody. They just slog away and don't even got a gun at home.

Like Natalina's father, and others like him.

A lot of these people have had it up to here with us kids offing everybody.

So they ask the State to make laws against us — against minors, I mean.

They always say they got to change us. That we're not doing too good the way we are.

But you can't just erase us and start all over!

You need to let a little of us stay as is.

Otherwise, our moms won't recognize us no more when we get out.

And they'll reject us.

And then we'll be lost again and start stealing and killing, cause we always turn to shit, and this time we won't even have our moms who love us!

So change us, but only a little.

And the decent people, they got the politicians on their side. Who think of them first!

You want my opinion, them in the law ought to think about all of us in Nisida first.

Then the women like my mom, then those who're doing a little better but not really, then the beggars and addicts.

And not people like Ciro.

Him, the laws are in his favor, and he don't deserve it.

Teach, you want to know what Ciro Varriale's got on his arm? A tattoo of the *Maronna*. So that Jesus Christ, when Ciro dies, will put him in Heaven, cause he's got a photo of Christ's mom on his arm.

But Jesus Christ ain't stupid!

You ask me, Ciro's going to Hell, and we'll see each other there.

That I promise!

And I'll spit in his face for everything he done, specially to me and my mom.

Me, I know I'm going to Hell for killing that guy whose last name I don't remember, just that his first name's Michele.

Teach, you say it ain't true we're going to Hell, that there's hope for everybody and Hell's not a place for children. Minors ain't allowed.

You ask me, you only say this cause you're good and you're afraid of these sorts of things.

You, you're never going to Hell, not even on a visit, like you do here. They just don't let your kind come close, cause you even love people like us.

But I ain't scared of this sort of thing.

I ain't got the right, like I already told you.

So I expect I'll be headed to Hell, and I accept it.

Can't be any worser than the life I had before I died.

The penguin tells me I got to repent for all the awful things I done, and then maybe (maybe!) they'll put me in Purgatory, where dead people go that God ain't sure where to put yet, cause there ain't room for everybody in Heaven.

Yeah, right.

And I'll just sit there like a total loser.

No, I'd rather not repent and head straight to Hell where there's always plenty of room for all the dead, so there won't be no trouble finding me a spot.

Sometimes I do think about it, though, to tell the truth.

About Heaven.

And the angels there, I've never understood if they're born angels, or if they were people first, like everybody else.

Teach, you're always saying you're sure I'll be going there, to Heaven.

You're better than a penguin when you say this, and maybe you picked the wrong profession. But you're too beautiful to be a nun—there, I said it, but I won't say it again.

So I gotta ask: when you say I'm going to Heaven, do you mean it for real, or are you maybe teasing me a bit and trying to make me feel a little calmer?

You really think they'll still take me up there, even though I killed that guy named Michele?

Or will they ask me to change, like them with their laws?

And what if they just change me directly, from up there?

But I don't want to change, Teach.

Come on now.

I'll still be "me" even when I'm dead.

Ain't that true?

Yesterday someone arrived from Bologna who don't speak our language cause he's Italian.

That meant going after him. Me, first, cause that's how you learn to get by.

I came up to him and asked who he belonged to, but he didn't understand.

Then I asked him how much time he got, and he said he was still waiting on his trial and didn't know.

I made sure he understood I was in charge here, cause *aggio accis' a uno*—I killed somebody—and that ain't no small thing. And I patted him, no big deal, just a warning.

But this guy, he stared at me and said he killed somebody too, his father, and I just stood there looking like some asshole, *'nu strunz'*.

This kid's father was from Naples, but his mother's from Bologna. That don't happen so much here in Nisida, cause, cept for Abdu, we all belong to Neapolitan families through our mothers, our fathers, our grandmas and grandpas, and everybody before that, though I don't know what them are called.

Anyway, this Bolognese who just arrived is named Arnoldo Francesco de Falco, that seems like a made-up name, but it ain't in the least.

I said right then that I'm calling him Totò, cause it's simpler, and he said: Okay.

Totò killed his father last week. Stabbed him twice.

His father was a lawyer, a real court lawyer, not like the guy who defended me. A regular lawyer, not super rich, not super old, cause there are lawyers out there who're young and just scraping by, not like dentists and *Mafiusi*.

Totò's mom took her dead husband's side from the get-go. Said her son was a murdering piece of shit and that's an awful thing to hear, even if it's true.

Totò confessed, cause he says it was self-defense.

But who's gonna believe him?

Me, sure, but not the judges, and they put him in jail like they done all of us.

I tried to comfort him, cause it was self-defense for me too, with Michele. But here I am all the same. And I remembered when I first came to Nisida, not knowing nobody.

So I told him now he was starting his second life here.

You'll see Totò, Teach, when he starts school in January, he's just come and needs to settle in. Plus, there's no seats available in school now, not till the end of the year, so he's gotta wait. I told him I'd introduce him to all the teachers, but you're the best here, with all respect to them others who ain't worth shit.

I liked this guy right off, cept he comes from Bologna, and that's up North but I guess not by much. So then I introduced him around, so he'd feel better, cause when you know people's names you're less scared. I had him meet everybody: Marietto, Carmine, Rinuccio, another three guys.

Tonino 'o Bulldog was there too, but I didn't introduce him.

But he came over and shook Totò's hand anyway. Told him his first and last name.

Then he looked at me.

And this time he talked too.

Said him and me don't need no introductions cause my face says it all, and maybe he remembered me.

I answered that my face don't say nothing to nobody without my say-so, and that goes for him too.

But he just went on, said my name was Zeno.

With a last name of Iaccarino.

Him and me, neither of us had time to say nothing else cause Corradino was coming at us like a tractor and saying:

"My name's Corrado Palumbo and if the name Zeno means something to you, mine's gotta mean even more."

Well, seeing how the name Palumbo means something to every one of us, Tonino all of a sudden couldn't remember my name no more. He left, but gave me a long look first.

I wanted to kill him.

Corradino said not to worry about Tonino 'o Bulldog. He don't got no balls, scared of a fag like him.

The whole day, Corradino was happy cause he'd been "the man."

He felt great and he pranced around all of us, even the *surveglianti*, cause he'd defended me, a murderer, but also his friend.

And I let him, cause he needed it, and I liked seeing him telling everybody this big thing he done.

Made him think back to when he was a real *Camorrista*, and that felt good.

But then he remembered about Pompei and his father.

Then he remembered his mom.

And Corradino went back to being a kid.

But I like him that way too.

A while back it was the Day of the Future.

That's right: of the future.

I come to understand it was the day the Warden clears his conscience and does some ball breaking, though we got better things to do.

We were in the large hall where they also hold Mass.

He was there and so was the social worker who don't actually help nobody with their case cause it ain't her problem.

The Warden spoke to us about this "future" I ain't never seen, but that's normal, cause the future's tomorrow, not today.

Said the "future" is our life outside, if and when we get out alive.

He invited a whole bunch of people to this, cause really he's shameless.

All regular people, not like us. People with diplomas and all the right papers.

There was a doctor, a soccer player for Afragolese, someone with a *trattoria* in Margellina, someone who owned a scrapyard in Fuorigrotta.

You ask me, the Warden paid them to come here.

They all talked about their work.

Then the Warden asked us what we want to do for a living, like you ask us, Teach, but he does it cause he's required by law.

And I thought maybe I'd say I want to be a writer, cause that's what I told you, and also cause it's true.

But I was afraid they'd all make fun of me.

And that it wasn't no real job anyway, not like a doctor or soccer player.

So I kept my mouth shut.

None of the others knew what to say neither, cause what kind of ideas do you come up with in prison? Your ideas are in prison too.

So no one spoke up.

And the Warden got pissed, cause we were making him look bad. He said we were a bunch of losers and that we got shit for brains.

That's what he said: "You got shit for brains!"

And it's not like a prison warden should talk like that! But it ain't my fucking business—he can say what he wants.

Then one of the guys, named Lino, who's in here for armed robbery and some unarmed robbery besides, this Lino took it personal cause the Warden's somebody who needs to learn some manners.

And this Lino gets up in front of everybody and says right in the Warden's face that he wants to be a pimp with a bunch of whores and his business out on the sidewalk.

And we all start laughing.

Even the doctor and the soccer player.

But not the Warden or the social worker, who just put her hands over her face.

And then I said, if I was a woman, I'd work for Lino and get my mom to work for him too. Cause the way I see it, Linuccio's got a talent for this kind of thing and he'd make all of them into high-class hookers, practically like regular ladies going to the hairdresser and everything.

The Warden didn't even get the chance to stand up and tell us we all sucked before Carmine jumped onto his chair. He shouted: "Me, I wanna be in charge of the gypsies, like them in Piazza Dante, just like them!"

He said he'd learn them to beg. Then he'd pocket all the money and only give them what they need to eat and drink.

He didn't say this cause he's a racist. Carmine's not a bad guy, you know that, Teach. He only said it cause there's so many of them gypsies wandering around just waiting on somebody to make good use of them, so he benefits and so do they and everybody's happy.

Well, the Warden punished us for all this craziness: we had to go back to our cells and he took away our activities and all the other nice or normal things we got in here.

We were shut up for one whole day.

We were dying to get out.

We couldn't even go to school, though that ain't exactly fun.

So I took the time to write a little, Teach, and drew some pictures to go with it.

I drew my island.

Then I did a writer with money and books and a pen in his hand.

Then my mom and our place.

I don't know how to draw, just like I don't know how to write. Pretty much the same.

I'd like to know how. Cause then I can paint a portrait of my Natalina. I ain't got no photo of her, and I'm forgetting her a little. And it makes me sad.

But you know how to draw, so maybe you could do it for me?

Pe' favore?

I'll describe her, you can draw her, and then I can put it up in my cell.

Natalina's a little cross-eyed, but she ain't ugly.

She's got dark hair like me, but I'm taller.

And she's always got on the same dress, pink with green flowers. Her father can't scrounge up nothing better. She's also got a coat, camel-colored. It was her dead mom's.

But don't draw her with the coat, cause I don't like winter and I want to remember my summer Natalina.

This morning was visiting hour.

On these days, I always feel crappy.

I ain't seen my mom in forever.

She don't got the time to come for visits. No, that ain't true. Mom's got the time but not the money for the bus. And nobody'll drive her. We ain't never had a car. I had my scooter, but it got stole — seized. But Mom don't know how to drive one anyway.

When the others go down to see their relatives, I always feel kind of sad, and I'd also like to punch out them who got family and money, more than I got.

Me, I've had one visit only, when Vittoria was here.

That was last year. She was already carrying her second, and she come in with a big belly and sweating like a horse. She said it was the pregnancy, but it looked to me like she was just sweating.

We hadn't seen each other for years and years, not since way before I been in here. She seemed different, all dressed up.

I remember when she was little. She saw me, and she come and hugged me and touched my cheek, and it almost felt like she was our mom.

She said I was handsome but didn't mean it.

She said she was expecting another boy. She wanted a girl, but it's not like she could just chuck this one. She said she wanted to call him Zeno, but he'd be Donato. Then she showed me a photo of her first, who's ugly like his father, but I kept my mouth shut on that.

Vittoria told me I really grew, and it surprised her. I said people grow, no big deal.

I asked her to say hello to our mom for me. But she couldn't, they ain't close no more, she tells me, don't talk at all.

Then she said that God alone knew how much she suffered for me, for Mom, for Dad, and for all our kind. But God never told me nothing about it, just kept it to himself. So all this suffering, I ain't never seen or heard it.

Then she left, cause she had to catch three buses to get back home.

She said she'd send me some money, if she could, but I told her to give it to Mom, who needs it more than me. She said okay, but you want my opinion, she didn't send nothing to nobody, cause it ain't up to her anyway.

When I went back to my cell, I felt crappier than ever and I'm glad she ain't come back.

She wrote me a letter, sometime after that. She said the same stuff as before and asked me to write her, when I felt like it. But there wasn't no return address. So I never did.

During visiting hour, I always just lay on my bed.

And Corradino's there with me, and this, this loneliness, is always better with two than by yourself.

Nobody in his family comes and visits Corradino and gives him a kiss, cause his father won't allow it. He told everybody his son's dead to him. But that ain't true — Corradino's very much alive. But he is alone.

He wants to see his mom again, but he can't. He wants to see his boyfriend. I think he even kind of wants to see his father, but he never says it.

Just today he told me when he gets out he's coming to visit me at least once a week, if the judge lets him. He says he's coming so often, I tell him to stop coming cause he's such a pain.

Then he got a little sad, cause he's older'n his age.

He looked at the ceiling like somebody was up there and told me the fish merchant, the guy he loves, is named Giggi, with two gs.

I was glad to hear it, not that it was information I could use.

Then he started looking out the window like a real grown-up, and I went and stood beside him.

In Forcella, in my place with my mom, there's no window. Just a door.

Which ain't the same thing.

I mean it.

A window's totally different.

I never had my own window before. I always just looked out other people's.

So one nice thing about prison: there's enough windows for everybody.

I'm real bad.

But not on the inside.

I'm bad on the outside, cause I done real ugly things.

But these things stay on the outside—I don't know if I'm making any sense, and if you don't get what I'm saying, I can try writing it again.

I ain't the things I done.

Well, them things too.

The judges, they never understood. Cause that's who they are. And it ain't like you can change them.

That's their job.

They don't understand, and they punish everybody. I don't know if when they get home they punish their wives too, or if they just save it for court.

Maybe at home they can't decide.

Not with me though.

It was September 18, I'll never forget, when they decided on my sentence, and with all them sentences for a kid, they decided on the longest.

I mean, the way longest.

And I can't appeal it neither—it's final.

I won't tell you how long I got cause it'll upset you.

But maybe you know, Teach, maybe I can see it in your eyes.

The judges didn't give a fuck if I was a juvenile—they judged me like I was a grownup.

They said I didn't have no remorse.

But how could I—my life was in danger, and also, I got my pride.

I didn't want to die, and that ain't something you can really control. Just like breathing.

So when I get out of jail, I'll still be young, sort of.

And I don't know if I'll get the time to do all the things I really want to do in life.

Like travel and see a bunch of beautiful places.

Even if I was free, I couldn't visit nothing, cause I got my responsibilities and not much money.

But if I was born in a different time, I'd of become a discoverer of people and countries, like that guy who invented the Americans.

What's his name?

And I'd of invented people who are way better and not such ballbreakers.

I'd of discovered *'nu bellu paese*, a beautiful country, big, peaceful, where the weather's always sunny, even at night. *'Nu bellu paese*, where all the grownups are in jail and the world is ours.

Sure, some adults can be out of prison, but on permanent probation or under house arrest.

You can be out, Teach, don't worry!

Cause the way I see it, you still think like a child, and that's why you're so kind.

Christopher Columbus. That's his name.

Anyway, when I do get out of here, I won't have time to discover nothing.

The social worker who don't help nobody said I'll need a job right away.

And not a job I like.

Just a job.

I'll have to find work super quick. And it'll probably pay bad, like you're paid, Teach.

And I'll be free. And starving to death.

But right now, that ain't my problem, that's a long ways off, too many days to start counting down.

Anyway, while I serve my sentence, I want to get off Nisida.

I wish I had four wheels under me, like a car.

Or maybe oars like a boat.

And then I might get to see something around me.

Maybe I could visit the world, even in here, go ahead with my travels.

For example, I'd like to see the ocean, cause it's older and bigger than the sea, so it's got more to say. I'd like to visit the Chinese, Arabs, Blacks in Africa. I'd also like to meet the English and their queen, to see if they're real or if they're just in the movies. And then I'd like to go see my Natalina at her place. Cause then I can kiss her again, after all this time. And I ain't forgotten how. Never!

You want to know the truth, Teach?

I wish I'd been born an explorer. So I could visit everything.

Or at least been born with a bit more luck.

Or maybe not born at all.

But most of all, I wish I'd been born a child. But I wasn't ever that lucky—they made me be grown up, right from the start.

In here, they say we're "minors," another way of saying we're children but that won't upset people on the outside.

But this island's still a prison, it ain't fooling nobody.

Me, I never believed in Babbo Natale. And not the Befana, neither, not even when I was *piccirillo*. Cause how're you supposed to believe in something that don't exist?

But you always bring us a stocking on January 6, though it ain't allowed, and Franco helps you under the table and you stuff our stockings with hard candies and chocolates and even sweet coal and walnuts.

You're our Befana, Teach, no disrespect—you ain't no witch—you're beautiful!

Let's say you got the job and heart of the Befana, but not the face.

And then Franco, last year, he dressed up like Babbo Natale.

They even make us Christmas dinner in here, on Christmas Eve.

But just cause they feel sorry for us, not cause they really mean it.

Then they make you go sit through the priest's Mass at midnight to celebrate Jesus's birthday.

But it's required, and nobody really wishes him a happy birthday.

Then last year at midnight, after Mass, Franco came, and it wasn't even his shift, and he brung us gifts, stuff to eat, candy mainly, but we didn't mind in the least!

You could tell it wasn't Babbo Natale, just Franco.

Well, anyway, the real one don't exist.

Franco exists more than him.

But don't tell your little girl, who was born a child. She still gets to believe in bullshit.

The other day me and Tonino 'o Bulldog finally got to talking.

We were in the common room and that stinking asshole comes up to me like he done before.

He sat down real close, cause Corradino wasn't there.

I started getting up, but he looked at me with that bastard face of his.

So I just sat back down again, on principle.

He asked me if I belonged to Luigi Iaccarino, and I said yeah, he's my dad and he's doing time in Bergamo.

He told me the name of his *vicolo* in Forcella. Said it was real close to mine and I couldn't not know it.

Then he asked if I had a girl named Natalina Marrazzo and I didn't say yes or no.

Then he grinned at me, just like the piece of shit he is.

He said he knew who I was, and he remembered me.

I was the son of a whore and Luigi Iaccarino. And I sold drugs for Ciro Varriale. And I was a purse-snatcher. And I killed somebody and that's why I was here. He said in

Forcella, my name comes up once in a while. Sometimes for something bad, sometimes for something good.

Then he looked me in the eye and told me Natalina's not there no more.

She left Forcella. Married some guy from Pallonetto, not in the Camorra, and he's a loser, totally broke. Not a criminal though. His first name's Bernardo, he couldn't remember his last name.

And now they lived outside Naples, in Frattamaggiore. Together.

And Natalina's not my *'nnammurata* no more, she's somebody else's, and he's better than me, cause he's free.

He said if Natalina married him, that could only mean one thing, and I knew it too.

And now everybody else knew it.

And then I fucking punched him.

In the face.

My Christmas furlough, I only thought about it afterwards.

That I'd lost it, and I'd been hoping for it so much, and for what, for nothing, like always happens to people like me. And I wouldn't get to see my mom, I'd never see her again. But God the Father loves me, cause 'o *survegliante*, he didn't see it happen. Tonino returned to his cell, not saying nothing to nobody, cause he ain't got the balls.

And him, wanting me to believe all that shit he said.

But I ain't gonna give him the satisfaction. He ain't worth it. I'm somebody in Nisida and Tonino, he ain't nobody and that's all he'll ever be, even if he is older.

And I know my Natalina's waiting just for me and she ain't nobody else's.

Teach, last month you said I should write her a Christmas letter. And tell her I still love her and always think about her. Then she won't forget me and be with nobody else.

And she'll wait for me.

But *io nun tengo 'o curaggio*—I'm scared.

I don't want her to answer.

And I don't want her to not answer.

You say I'm being an ostrich, hiding my head in the sand.

That ain't nothing.

If I could, I'd be the whole damn zoo.

And I don't want to know if what Tonino 'o Bulldog says is the truth.

I want it to be a lie, and him a liar.

I don't know if I'll get to see my Natalina when I'm out for Christmas.

But for now, it's better that way.

I thought about it yesterday, all night. I didn't sleep. And I didn't tell nobody, not even Corrado, cause I wasn't in the mood.

I ain't never suffered for love, and I don't plan to.

It's too big a hurt and I already got myself plenty of hurt. I'd rather get life in prison than this thing here.

I don't know if when somebody loves, the other's obliged to love them back, or if there's some law against that.

And if so, then I'm also illegal in love.

And then I really don't got no hope.

What saves me in here is my thoughts and memories that

are beautiful, even if they're made up—but who's gonna know, anyway?

Thinking about my Natalina, I just have to do it, have to think about her.

Same with my mom.

But Mom's the present. Natalina's the future—she's "after."

Natalina is this:

When I get out, I marry her and we have a regular life, like everybody else. A regular home, on the second floor, not the street, with an eat-in kitchen, kids, a TV, chairs, a couch, curtains, all that.

I know Natalina can find somebody better, cause I ain't stupid. And that would really please her dad, Sabatino Marrazzo, *'nu brav' omm'*, it would make him super happy.

She could find a better man than me, respectable, somebody who ain't been in jail, somebody free.

But the love I can give her, even in jail, is way better than that free guy will ever give her.

Cause it's crazy love, and there ain't nothing better.

In here, I only think of her.

Nothing else.

But that guy on the outside who's legal, he's got his mind on all sorts of things. Work, relatives, friends.

Not me.

There ain't nothing on my mind.

Just her.

So maybe I should of said that to Tonino 'o Bulldog, stead of pounding him in the face. Should of explained it.

Like you're always saying, Teach, hitting don't solve nothin.

Better to always talk and talk and talk. Even with a *sciem'* like Tonino.

But what I should be saying, it don't come to me right away.

It only comes later.

While the bullshit, that always comes right on time.

Christmas in Nisida don't exist and, if it does, it's bad.

We're not real happy in December. We feel it, being in here, even more than the other months.

Me, though, this December, I'm crazy happy, not like last year.

And the others are a little jealous.

Cause I got my furlough and at least one Christmas, like we all should, like we all got a right to. So I started my countdown, like they do at New Year's, cept it's days.

And I really got to thank you, Teach, cause you got me my permission.

You told the Warden, the magistrate too, that I'm 'nu bravu kid and maybe you really think so — depends on the day.

I sure hope you're right saying it, but I ain't so sure.

Well, you go ahead and believe it, cause you're a good person, and you love us, and I love you too, Teach.

Today's December 20, December 20 exactly, and I get out on the 24th.

So today is minus four.

And who cares if it's only two days, Christmas Eve and Christmas, I'll still be home, at my place, and that's always better than a cell on an island.

Then on the night of the 25th, Franco and the other officer will bring me back, but I'll still have everything I seen, ate, said.

Teach, when you see me again in January, you won't even recognize me!

I can't wait to see Christmas again, and maybe I already told you, but I'll always keep saying it.

Cause Christmas is Christmas, and that sure ain't Easter.

At my place, when I was still *piccirillo*, Mom couldn't even put up a tree, on account of the money.

But to make me and Vittoria happy, she hung some garland on our *vascio* door, stuck on with tape. Then we forgot about it and it's the end of summer and it's still on the door. So she looks at us and says, "In only a few months it'll be Christmas again!" and she left it up till the following Christmas.

That was so great.

But me and Vittoria gave our poor mom hell.

We really wanted a tree, and we especially wanted a Nativity scene, cause we were little kids, and we wanted to play with the shepherds.

But it cost too much and Mom just couldn't do it.

So when I really wanted to see Nativities, I'd walk along San Gregorio Armeno, that wasn't too far from us.

Walking up that road, I'd look at all them shepherds and the *Maronne* and San Giuseppi and babies in mangers.

They were all the same, all crammed into bowls, like hazelnuts and walnuts instead of saints.

Some Nativities were so huge that me, Mom, and Vittoria could of slept in them easy.

I was a little jealous of the shepherds and Jesus too, cause even if he was born in a stall and had to end up like he did, he was fixed better than us.

I looked at all the figures in the Nativities that were always there: the shepherds with their sheep, Benino, who didn't give a shit and was fast asleep, the musicians, pizza makers, washerwomen, fruit vendors, the baker, fishermen fishing in the rivers with fake water, and the guy roasting chestnuts and selling them for lots.

I seen all the jobs in the world in those Nativities.

And then I saw the most important figures, not as funny, cause that ain't really their job, being funny: 'a Maronn' with her husband Giuseppe, the animals, a little baby, and the angels.

When I come back from my walk, I was always happy!

I'd tell Mom I saw the Nativities! That musk smell! And I listed all the figures, one by one.

But Mom gave me a sad look.

She didn't say nothing, cause she knows Nativities never got room for a whore.

And that don't seem fair to me, cause it's a job like any other, and even a whore's got a right to become a shepherd.

In the end, I was glad we couldn't afford no Nativity in our home.

So she wouldn't feel left out.

My mom's always got to feel equal, whatever makes her happy, cause she deserves it like anything.

Just now Franco's come to see us cause his uncle died, but he didn't much like his uncle, so he didn't give a shit that he died. He only went to the funeral to get a card, a photo, to give to Corradino for his collection. The card was an excuse — it's just as well this uncle kicked it when he did.

Franco came cause Corradino's so upset lately.

He's getting out in February, and it's coming up and it's for good, not like my furlough. His is for real. And seeing how he don't think like a delinquent no more, maybe Corradino won't wind up in jail no more. So if he can't be in here, he's got no choice but to be out there. He's happy to get out, but he's worried too.

Corrado, when he gets out of Nisida, he'll be a ghost, cause he's dead to his father. And if he goes back to Pompei, he'll be dead for real.

He don't know where to go or what to do, cause ghosts can't work.

I wonder, Teach: how do you rehabilitate a ghost?

Two weeks, Corradino ain't slept and only prayed.

He asked me to pray too, but I ain't as inspired as him and don't got the skill for it.

He keeps praying to that whole photo collection of his, of the dead, and to his *Maronne* and prayer cards. He says at least one of these here'll get fed up and give him what he's asking for, and I mean, Corradino and all his praying, it's wearing everybody out.

The other day he told me, when he gets out, he'll try real hard to get ahold of Tania 'o Sciosciammocca, a tranny friend of his who lives on Corso Umberto.

He wrote a letter to Tania last week.

They met when Corrado was a *Camorrista* in Pompei, but Tania 'o Sciosciammocca wasn't a transvestite then, was dressed like a man and went by Giorgio.

Corrado says this Tania can get him into my mom's line of work and I don't like it, cause he could do better, and I love him. Maybe he could be a fortune teller and read actual cards, not soccer cards, and maybe even a crystal ball. He could be a pizza maker, a fruit vendor, even sell contraband. Or if he really wants to be a fag, he can play one on TV and make a pile of money.

But he said he felt like going to Tania's and still being a tranny, but just at home. On the street, he wouldn't dress up.

I said they sometimes kill *femminielli*, specially when they're doing the work of real women. And even if he was a ghost, he was still alive and had better be careful.

But he answered he didn't have no other ideas, that a fortune teller's not a real job, it don't pay much, and there ain't a whole lot of customers. And his release date's coming up.

Then he asked me if my mom knows somebody who could be his pimp, but I can't help with that, cause Mom works on her own.

Plus I don't even know if she's still a whore, and can only tell him when I see her, cause that's how this kind of job goes.

Corrado said when he gets out, he'll go see her, my mom, he wants to meet her. He says from the way I talk about her she's a real mom, a little like his, but poorer. He wants to refresh his memory on moms, to see if he can still tell who they are on the street, or if he's lost his touch.

He also said if he makes a little money with Tania 'o Sciosciammocca, he'll give Mom some, cause with me in jail, she's gotta be in trouble.

Truth is, before what happened with me, my mom's troubles left with my father. If it was me, I'd of never gotten with him. I'd rather be an old maid for life. Even if he was the last man in the city.

But not her. She was stuck on him and nobody could make her change her mind.

Not that she didn't have no other choices.

There was a whole bunch of guys chasing after her, back when she didn't charge nothing.

Because she was beautiful, crazy beautiful, like an actress, better even. Them women are beautiful cause they got money to burn, but my mom didn't have nothing.

So she could of had somebody normal, somebody who treated others good. And could give her a life with money, so she wouldn't have to kill herself working, and go hungry like she does.

But then I wouldn't of been born. Or maybe I'd of been born somebody else and not Zeno. And that other guy would be happier than me, that's for sure.

But Mom was really in love with my dumbass dad.

He beat her.

And she didn't give a shit.

She pretended like it was nothing, like slaps and kicks don't hurt, but that was crap, cause she ain't a robot.

And my father beat us too.

He liked to punch real hard and it didn't make no difference if it was her or us, if we were little or not.

He even hit me when I was real *piccirillo*, one or two years old even. And I got the scars to prove it, from when I didn't remember yet. The other times, I remember them all.

But my mom, even with the beatings, still loved my father.

And me and Vittoria, we had hereditary love, and that's worse than being in real love. Watch out for that!

It's nice being a parent. Easy!

Cause you don't have to give a shit about your kids and can pretend like you never had them.

But us sons and daughters, we're here for good, and we gotta carry this cross our whole lives.

Like me and Corradino.

Truth, though?

It would of been better not being born a son.

Unfortunately, it's required.

And even if my father's a *strunz'*, I can't help but love him.
Cause it's normal to love your father.
And I was born very normal.
I was only born a little wrong.
And my heart, unfortunately, is right.

Tomorrow's minus one!

It's too good to be true, I just gotta write it down.

Late in the afternoon yesterday, the Warden came and threatened me, so that means I'm really getting out, and soon.

The Warden said if I do any crap while I'm out, he's calling on the members of Parliament he knows and making them reinstate the death penalty. Just for me.

I said there ain't no need cause there won't be no problems, that I'll behave myself and come back, but not to respect him. For Franco, cause he's responsible for me. And for you too, Teach, giving me this beautiful thing, cause you put in a good word from the beginning, even with some of the things I wrote here.

Franco, last night, he came to our cell and said he's happy to be meeting my mom, after everything I told him.

He said he knows, even if he ain't met her, that she's a good woman. Cause she had to do it all on her own, specially her two kids.

And to him, people shouldn't raise kids alone—it takes company.

Franco says my mom's brave, cause kids can make anybody lose their shit and take off.

But not her.

She stuck it out.

Franco promised he's buying a Christmas star, and it'll be from me, though I can't pay.

We'll bring it the day after tomorrow, when I get out.

So it's like I get to give a gift for free!

And my mom'll be super glad, I know it.

Someday, I'll give her a real, paid gift. I mean with clean money. But that'll have to wait, cause I ain't got no money at all right now, clean or *zozzoso*.

When I get out permanent, I'm finding a real job, I promise, Teach, maybe become a writer, like you want.

Make a shit ton of money.

And I'll buy Mom flowers, smiles, gold jewelry, a home, respect, and everybody being jealous.

In here, everybody's wanting me to talk about Christmas soon as I'm back.

Marietto came to me saying I need to remember *per filo e per segno* every last thing I eat on the 24th and 25th. He wants to know super precise: every taste and smell, breakfast, lunch, and dinner.

He also wants me to tell him what my mom says to me, after all this time. And to see if I still look the same, like before I was in here.

And so I feel like one of them TG reporters.

And I'm getting my memory ready. So I can keep everything in my head that I see. Then I'll make a list when I'm back in here.

But right after, I'm erasing my memories. I don't want to miss them too much, cause they'll be out there, and I'll be back in here.

Yesterday, Corradino loaned me a nice shirt, one of his. So I'll look good for Mom. He said if I bring it back all *zuzzosa* and dirty, he'll spit in my eye. Then he gave me a kiss and I'd of rather dodged it, cause we ain't got the same preferences, but in the end I didn't say nothing.

Anyway, seeing how today ain't exactly Christmas but a bit before, this morning we had a little performance.

Teach, don't feel bad you didn't see it, cause you were already on vacation.

Plus they took pictures they'll put in the *Mattino* and so we'll look like national douchebags.

Anyway, I'll tell you about it now.

Super quick, we put together a sort of live Nativity scene, with a choir and singing angels.

Definitely a live Nativity, but still without no whores.

Even the mayor came.

And he brung a bodyguard cause he's scared of all of us. You ask me, he's scared of the Warden too, cause the Warden's got an ugly face.

You know, the mayor almost looked like a normal guy.

And here he is, the boss of the city.

So, anyway, for the Nativity, I was 'o *zampugnaro*, along

144

with Totò 'o Bolognese. But we didn't have no bagpipes, cause they don't exist in Nisida. We had flutes.

They made Corradino a Magi and not the Madonna, cause maybe he'd feel like he was being made fun of. It was Lino played the *Maronna* instead, and he's even got a beard, but he ain't sensitive. Peppiniell' 'o scem' we made San Giuseppe, cause they got the same name. Abdu, who's Black, he was Melchior, one of the Magi who comes from Africa, so they matched. Rinuccio, who's nuts, was just decoration. He was the comet and even if he shook some it didn't matter, cause the star with the tail moved too. Marietto played a sheep.

In the end we pissed ourselves laughing.

It was so great being on stage, like we were saints and angels and stars.

Don Vicienzo was there too, cause it was required.

He sat up front, disgusted—seeing all the damned and criminals in the Nativity was total torture for him! But he had to just sit there and take it. He didn't get a say.

And we thought it was so funny, seeing him dying out there. So at least we could spoil Christmas for him a little, cause it's when a priest earns the most.

The mayor clapped after our songs.

The Warden too, but it was pretend clapping.

Then the mayor said goodbye, at a distance.

And he shook the Warden's hand and kissed the priest's hand, and that was super gross, cause Don Vicienzo ain't no beauty!

Then the mayor had some pictures taken to make sure

he gets reelected by the people living in shit neighborhoods who maybe also got a kid or brother here in Nisida.

If he can show he's thinking about us too, then our relatives will vote for him.

Maybe they hope he'll get us out early.

But that won't happen, cause the law's got it in for us and the mayor don't decide nothing about sentencing. He's only got jurisdiction on the streets.

Anyway, the mayor came here all slick and ready.

Didn't even have to go to our play. Just to the prison.

He had on a watch worth more than all of Nisida. Everybody in here wanted to cut his arm off, but we couldn't do nothing about it and just had to keep our mouths shut.

Me, I wanted to talk to him a little on my own, not to say nothing mean or even steal something.

But the Warden kept the mayor away from us, afraid we'd insult him. He said if we so much as tried to talk to the mayor, he'd do us an injury.

So nobody said nothing, and just like the mayor came, he was gone again.

Went back to where he lives, not some shit neighborhood. A normal place, with buildings, streets, all that.

And I didn't get a chance to ask him a thing or two, just out of curiosity.

I'd of liked to ask him if he really lived in Naples, or else in Milan.

And if he was a politician for real or just the mayor.

Cause if he's a politician for real, maybe he can change the laws and get me out a little early.

And this could be a nice gift for my mom.

Or else, if the mayor's scared to get me out early, maybe he can give my mom an address, so I can write her some letters, even if she don't know how to read.

And last, if he's mayor and can do mayor things, does that mean he can put some kind of number on our door?

Any number.

We'd even take a zero.

MINUS ONE

Today's the last day before my leave.

And thank God—*'assa 'a Maronn' e tutti i santi!*

Tomorrow'll be the best day of all.

Wish it could go on forever, but it just can't.

Teach, I'm leaving you everything I wrote before I go, so you can read it whenever you please when you're back in January, after La Befana.

I'm giving my pages to Franco, who's *'nu brav' omm'* and he can even read them, if he wants. I don't mind.

Cause I ain't written nothing bad, right?

I am dying to see Christmas again, and I know I keep saying it, but it's true!

You see Christmas out there and don't notice, cause for you it's normal, but it ain't. It's special.

In here the good guards, them with a conscience, they put up a tree for us, but not with garlands, cause they're scared we'll kill ourselves, like Gaetano the Innocent.

So our tree's only got balls on it, plastic ones. They get squashed, just like our hopes.

I want to see a big tree for once, a tree reaching up to the sky, and covered in glass balls, balls that can break—like ours.

So I sure hope I get to see one like that tomorrow, in the middle of the street.

And I am dying to see Forcella again!

With all the Christmas lights and garlands, and jam-packed with all the people that are outside every day, every year.

And I'll see the decorations in the *vicoli*, and smell the roasted chestnuts!

Man, I sure hope Mom is dying to see me too, and that she's cooked something good to eat, for me and for Franco. Even though she ain't got the money. But maybe she saved up a little for me coming.

And I sure hope she don't look older. If she does, it'll scare me. But even if she's gotten super old, I'll pretend it's nothing and act like I don't care, so she won't feel bad.

Listen, Teach, I want to thank you again, in writing.

Cause the way I see it, if it wasn't for you, I'd be having another Christmas in jail.

And Merry Christmas to you, and your daughter, still so little, lucky her, and to your husband and even your distant relatives, if you got them and you get along, and if you don't get along, then them and all their dead can go to Hell before Christmas.

I sure hope you don't miss us too much during the holidays, but we'll see you in January, with those Befana stockings you bring us. Man, the Madonna sure must love you!

I bet you miss us, though.

But don't—for once, think about your own shit—sorry for the swearword.

But I bet you won't just think about yourself, cause you're super stubborn.

But you're always in here with us, even when you're out there. You're always close.

And when you can't sleep at night, even with it cooler, I'll think about you getting in your car and driving up to the top of Coroglio.

And stopping to take in the view.

You're there to look at Nisida. You can see it real well, this rotten island, and you think about us in here and you out there.

You feel guilty, and it don't seem fair to you.

But that ain't true, Teach—don't you let yourself think for one minute that I'm decent.

It's right the way it is.

We deserve what we got, and they had to put us in here.

And then I can see you, looking at the sea all around. That you like so much!

And you're thinking that to Zeno the sea just sucks, and that he'll never like it.

And then you feel bad, like always.

So I want to give you a Christmas present.

It's a surprise.

I looked at the sea all day yesterday, the other night too, and I didn't tell nobody, cause if I did they'd of copied me.

You're always telling us we gotta find something beautiful about the sea for ourselves. To find the poetry and the beauty in the sea.

So, for your gift, I found it for you:

You ask me, this sea is useless
But it does something after all.
The sea's trying to shift Nisida: it's trying with its
waves!
While here in prison, we're trying with our eyes.

So what do you think?

You like my poem?

The sea on one side, and us on the other: we're pushing, pushing, and pushing! But this old bitch won't ever budge, will just stay here!

And we're here too, feeling bad.

But in my view, the sea also feels kind of bad.

Everybody on the outside, the people you know too, they ain't got troubles, and when they look at the sea, what's there for them is boats, the port, fish, and all them dumbasses swimming in the water.

Them people: they're blind.

In the sea, there's also all our eyes trying to shift Nisida, but we just can't do it.

So you tell them, all them people on the outside that don't know: them in the water, they're swimming in our eyes and they gotta know that, and be respectful.

So that's your present, Teach, I sure hope you like it!

Because it's felt, but it ain't paid for.

But also: it ain't stolen.

Merry Christmas, happy new year, happy Befana, and all that.

The best to you and yours, and the worst to those you hate.

Your student,

ZENO IACCARINO

Madam dear,

I write you because I did not find your number in the phonebook. In Nisida we only have your address. So I am writing because the situation is serious.

Zeno is gone.

They shot him as soon as we arrived at his door yesterday.

We had to take care of his mom. We called the ambulance for her but not for him, because it was no use.

I am very sorry to give you this unpleasantness in writing, but I did not find your number in the phonebook. Maybe you are there under your husband's name.

Meanwhile the warden was on vacation and was not informing you.

I do not know if it was on the news because no one knew Zeno.

But you did, and so did I.
Let us hope that the Madonna knows him, too.
I pray she also forgives him.
Dear Madam.
Farewell.

Franco the guard

Author's Note

Any resemblance to actual people or events is entirely coincidental, though, really, I haven't written anything so bad here, have I?

True, the warden in Nisida at that time wasn't a terrible person. And the priest who worked with the boys wasn't a sewer—actually, he seemed like a very good man.

As for the teachers, inmates, and guards over the years, some were probably bastards and others decent, but I can't say for sure.

Pope John Paul II did come to Naples, but in 1990, not 1991.

When you go to Piazza del Plebiscito by way of Piazzetta Carolina, you will find a sculpture of a lion, but not with "*Z. e N. pe' semp*" on its rump. Instead, some Enzo carved his name and let everyone know he was born in 1979.

But certain things are true here, and the reader needs to know this: the island of Nisida can't be shifted, at least not with oars or a motor; people are born by chance and there's nothing you can do about it, no matter how hard you try; a window and a door aren't the same thing; if you do tarot readings with Panini *calcio* cards, Ciro Ferrara brings good luck no matter what, even if he is upside down.